I0533577

Tiny Tales:
Flash Fiction

5-Minute or Less Reads

for

Busy People

Susan Tuttle

Published by: WriterWithin Publications

All rights reserved. No part of this publication may be reproduced, stored in or introduced into a retrieval system, or transmitted in any form, or by any means (electronic, mechanical, photocopying, recording or otherwise), except for short quotes for review purposes only, without prior written permission of the publisher and copyright owner of this book.

This is a work of fiction. All characters and events in each of these stories are purely the imagination of the author. Any resemblance of any character to any person, living or dead, is merely coincidence.

Copyright © 2011-2018 Susan Tuttle

A WriterWithin Publication

ISBN: 1-941465-22-6

ISBN-13: 978-1-941465-22-6

WRITER
WITHIN

Dedication

This volume is dedicated to two of the most wonderful writers and people I've ever had the privilege to know, who have supported me in uncountable ways:

Anna Unkovich
and
Paul Alan Fahey.

They are sleeping with the angels now, inspiring us from above. I miss you both more than I can say.

Dedication.

Tiny Tales: Flash Fiction

Susan Tuttle

Contents

Tiny Tales: Flash Fiction

Susan Tuttle

INTRODUCTION

Back in 2011, I decided to try my hand at teaching fiction writing. Why? Because I had a bookshelf filled with "how to write" books that I wanted to read, but couldn't. I love mystery and suspense, sci-fi and fantasy; in fact, that's what I mostly read. And if someone doesn't die in the first chapter or two, I lose interest. Believe me, in those "how to write" books, no one ever dies— except maybe me, out of boredom.

So I started The *What If?* Writing Group and cracked those how-to books, eventually designing a series of lessons and exercises that would give me what I wanted to know and practice in my own writing. (It's amazing how many books *tell* you what to do, but don't show you *how* to do it. Mine do both; if you're interested, check out my series of six workbooks titled *Write It Right: Exercises to Unlock the Writer in Everyone*: www.WriterWithinPubs.com.

I may be "teaching" the classes, but I'm also there to learn and grow. I do all the exercises with my students. So you can imagine that, over the last seven years of teaching two weekly classes that encompass an average of two lessons per class, I have amassed a pile of short pieces, most of which, to my surprise, stand as stories of their own. Or, at least interesting scenes.

Here you'll find stories/scenes based on class exercises: a character, a setting, a given theme, a specific situation, a weird (but true) news report, a life experience, an opening line or phrase, or even a crazy number.

The shortest story/scene is only one page; the longest is six. None should take you more than five minutes to read. You can finish one at a stoplight (though I don't recommend reading if you're in the driver's seat!), when standing in line somewhere, waiting in the doctor's office, on lunch break, whenever. You can have fun with these tales and not deduct any appreciable time from your busy day.

Enjoy!
Susan

The Want of a Nail

It started with a broken nail.

Melissa had everything planned, all her ducks line up in a row, so to speak. Breakfast at six followed by her daily run through the park. Then shower, don her new outfit, spend a half hour at the makeup table to make herself presentable and off to the interview by eight, which gave her a half hour to spare, in case traffic got squirrelly. She'd lit her candles the night before, performed her good luck ritual, and slept the sleep of the innocent. The job was in the bag.

Until she broke a nail.

It happened when she slammed the door on her way to the park. She caught the edge of the jamb and heard a faint *crack!* But she didn't stop, didn't realize what had happened until she was partway through the run. The sun was just topping the trees, flooding her with warmth, when she paused, jogging in place, to take a sip from her water bottle. And saw the nail.

Snapped on a diagonal. Ragged. Bleeding a bit at the cuticle.

Her lungs froze. She stared at her hand in horror. Her right hand. Her shaking hands hand. The one she could not hide in a pocket or behind her back. The one everyone would see, especially the casting director. For the *nail* commercial.

This isn't happening! she thought. Her body began to tremor. Her vision darkened. Her breath came in huge gasps as she hyperventilated. A scream sounded deep within her and rose to block out everything else, until she couldn't hear the birds chirping, the breeze whispering, the thud of other runners' feet on the cinder path.

It's not real, she told herself. *Finish the run. When you get home everything will be all right.*

She forced herself to move, her steps halting and uneven, a half-run, half-stagger toward the bridge that crossed the ravine. She thought of last night's ritual, went over it in her mind. She'd done it right, she was sure of it. Smooth as silk, the black candles, the incense, the wand, the chant. Warding off evil and bad luck. But when she looked, her nail was still broken.

She screamed as she approached the apron of the wooden bridge. Her hands spasmed and she dropped her water bottle. It bounced and began to roll toward the drop off. Melissa lunged for it and skidded on the mist-damp boards. She fell hard, rapping her chin on the hard ground. Her teeth clicked together and pain shot into her jaw. She tasted blood in her mouth. She lay still a moment as shock skittered through her. Early morning bird song wrapped around her still form. The sun caressed her back. Tears flooded her eyes.

No! She couldn't cry. She'd have red eyes for the interview, she'd look like some horror film monster, not a hand and nail model. She took a deep breath and pushed herself to her knees, lifted her head. Warmth trickled down her chin and her fingers came away red when she swiped at it.

Great. Just what I need, she thought, exploring her swelling face with tentative fingers. *A split lip. This isn't fair!* Tears again threatened but she shoved them away and straightened her spine. Too bad. She's do her best with coverup and lipstick and let them think collagen. She wasn't about to let this ruin her chance for fame and fortune.

Melissa climbed to her feet, jogged in place a moment to reacquaint her muscles with movement, then set off across the covered bridge. Her steps echoed from the wooden ceiling above her. The breeze wafted down the length of the bridge, cooling her heated body. Her heartbeat evened out, her pace lengthened and she entered the zone where nothing intruded, where her spirit soared and everything seemed possible. She would rise above a broken nail and a split lip. She'd win the contract and the world would know her as The

Beauty Girl. She'd be famous, she'd be rich, she'd be loved and admired.

She grinned as the came off the bridge and turned right onto the cinder path. Her foot hit a stone, her ankle turned and she went down again. A lightning bolt shot up her leg and she twisted as she fell, landing hard on her left side. She heard something crack! Way louder than when her nail broke. Loud enough to pause the birdsong around her.

She shook her head and tried to push herself up, but pain shot into her left arm. She looked down and saw her hand hanging at a weird angle from a grossly swollen wrist. *No, no, no, no, no!* rang in her head, a scream trapped beneath the agony tearing at her. Half on her knees, she inched over to the nearest tree, clung to the bark and tried to stand. But she slipped on wet leaves, lurched to the right and began skidding down the hill toward the creek below.

She snatched one-handed at grass and bushes that came out of the ground like a needle slipping through silken fabric. The hill steepened and she began to roll. She hit rocks and tree stubs, picking up speed until she splashed into the water at the bottom. Joggers found her there an hour later, half-drowned, covered with cuts and bruises, groaning in pain from three broken bones. Three weeks later she watched on television as The

Beauty Girl—not her—smiled at the world from her first commercial.

Melissa had lost it all. Lost love and adulation. Lost fame and fortune. Lost out on the most important interview of her life. Lost out on her life's dream. All for the want of a nail.

Signature Salad

Amanda had just about finished chopping the ingredients for her special salad when Kevin asked if he could help. It was the one she called "rustic" because it contained heirloom tomatoes, scavenged lettuces and other organic ingredients.

She'd never before prepared it on the fly, so to speak, a thought that made her laugh since she was presently about 9,000 feet in the air in Kevin's plane. She would serve it to Kevin and his brother and sister-in-law who were accompanying them to the Colorado ski resort for a vacation. And David, the pilot, of course.

"Sure." She pointed with the knife. "You could chop the mushrooms for me."

Kevin folded his arms around her waist and pulled her against him, snuggling his chin at the point where her neck and shoulder met. His beard tickled and she shivered.

"I so love a woman with a knife," he murmured into her ear.

"Keep this up and Kurt and Leslie will get an 'X' rated flight," she said, turning around and pushing him away. "The mushrooms, please."

"Okay, just remember to put them on the side, since Leslie is allergic to them."

"Okay. I only got them for David but I thought maybe someone else might like some, too."

Amanda didn't usually put mushrooms in the salad; she had only included them because the pilot had requested the fungi. She'd picked up a small box of them from a new stall at the local farmer's market just before they left. She loved that they didn't look anything like those white, anemic, obviously urban-approved mushrooms sold at the grocery store. These were smaller, darker, more exotic looking, with long, winding stems. If she had to include mushrooms, she wanted them to at least look like they belonged in her signature "rustic" salad.

Kevin busied himself with his knife and in another ten minutes they served heaping plates of glistening salad on the small table at the back of the plane. Everyone exclaimed over the intricate taste sensations in the dish and polished their plates. Not until she was cleaning up did Amanda realize that no one had added any mushrooms to their salads.

Since she hated to throw them out, she put an extra scoop of the fungi on David's plate and took it up to the cockpit. Then she rejoined the others who were lounging in the luxurious leather seats Kevin had had installed when he'd bought the small plane. They were deep in a discussion of which trails were hardest to ski when the cockpit door burst open.

The pilot stood in the doorway, blocking access to the navigation equipment. Heavy breaths lifted his chest; his eyes shifted in his head like skittish cats. Kevin asked him what was wrong, but David didn't answer, just slammed and locked the cockpit door behind him. Kevin rose and tried to approach the man, but David fended him off with his fists. Kurt also tried to take the man down, but David fought like a mad man, with the strength of ten. He knocked out Kurt and broke Kevin's arm, ranting all the while that they were holding him captive. Amanda tried to reason with him, but David threatened to hit her, too, and she retreated to the last row of seats where Leslie was tending to Kurt.

David's t-shirt bore huge rings of sweat at the neck and under the arms. Blood dripped from his nose. He howled in rage, then tore off the shirt, kicked off his shoes and yanked off his socks.

"David, stop! What are you doing?" Kevin yelled, cradling his injured arm and cowering away from the mad man rampaging in the aisle, brandishing a knife. David ignored him and cut away his pants. Then he stopped and looked at them.

"I have to get out of here!" he shouted. Then he ran for the door and opened it. It was all the passengers could to to hold on and not be sucked out into the atmosphere.

"I'm free!" David crowed as he leapt from the plane.

Within minutes all four passengers had passed out from lack of oxygen. The pilotless plane wobbled, lost altitude, then nosedived into the side of a mountain. And a hundred miles away, residents of Big Fork, Wyoming, stared at the half naked man who sat, quite dead, at the top of the radio tower that had been erected not three months before. No one could figure out how he'd gotten up there. Not until the autopsy was performed did the medical examiner discover that the half-digested mushrooms in his stomach were poisonous.

Hearts

Kassandra looked into the mirror and sighed. Another show tonight. She was so tired. Tired of singing, tired of being in the spotlight. Tired of being who she was.

It had been fun at first, way back when she was young, having the world at her feet, even if the world was only East Jasper, Wyoming. She still remembered the night the cowboys had thrown gold coins at her as she danced and sang her way across the stage. Fifty dollars she had left after she'd greased the piano player's palm, and the saloon owner's. She'd felt so rich, thought she'd never have to work again. Funny how fast fifty dollars disappeared.

But she'd not had trouble finding another job. Her reputation had preceded her. Not because she was that great a singer—her voice was passable, sweet and lilting, but nothing better than a thousand other girls could do. No, it was because, on a whim and in defiance of her father, she had lifted her skirts above her knees and kicked to the ceiling. Knobby as they were, those knees and skinny shins had driven the cowboys wild. And made her an employable vocalist across the northwestern states, wherever the stage coach could carry her.

So long ago, she thought now. *Is there no end to it?*

She leaned toward the mirror, her kohl pot in her hand and saw him behind her. Joel. The only man who had made her heart race. Joel of the gray eyes and large hands, the slow smile and narrow hips. He wasn't real, she knew, just the product of her imagination. An illusion. One more ghost giving her courage to continue. He winked at her and gave a slight nod before he faded away. One more crazy vision to add the the multitude of Joel ghost-illusions compiled over the years.

Hurry, please, she thought now as she kohled her eyes, rouged her cheeks, and drew the heart— her signature. She'd been waiting ever so long for Joel's return. Long enough to tire of the travel, the tawdry saloons, the high kicks that weren't quite so high now, the songs that felt and sounded the same every night. Too long.

She could still feel his arms around her the night before he'd left for the mine.

"We'll have a little house just outside of town," he'd said. "With a white picket fence and daisies in the front yard. And we'll have four children, two boys and two girls. And a dog."

"And a cat? I love cats," she'd said. He'd laughed and caressed her cheek.

"Yes, *two* cats, how's that?" She'd squealed and kissed him. "And we'll go to San Francisco every year to see the ocean and walk in the fog. Would you like that?"

She'd gazed at him, her heart full of excitement and trepidation.

"What if we get lost in the fog? I've heard it's terribly thick. What if I lose you in the fog?"

"Never fear. I will always find you, because I will leave my heart with you." He leaned down and pressed his lips to her cheekbone. "Right there. I will always find my heart. No matter where you go, how far away. Always."

Then he'd left for the mine and she'd gone on to Ada Mills and danced and sang. And to Rustler, and Grant's Pass and Eugene, dancing and singing and waiting for Joel to find his heart. The first night after he'd left she'd traced the imprint of his lips on her face, then took the kohl and drew a heart. So he could find her. Always find her. His heart.

He had yet to come.

She rose from the makeup chair and straightened her costume. Time to go on. She took one last glance in the mirror, one last look at the heart on her cheek, then went out the door, weariness dragging at her shoulders, her feet.

Thirty years she'd been waiting, thirty years of courage, thirty years of loneliness, thirty years of hearts. Maybe tonight Joel would return to her. Maybe this would be the night she could finally rest.

Concrete Work

Wilson never walked to work, though he lived in DC, the one city in the US where a walk anywhere was a walk into history. His friends thought he was crazy. After all, Wilson was a lobbyist for the construction industry. He made his living hobnobbing with senators and congressmen, glad-handing for the media and slapping the Vice President on the back. If anyone should walk to work, it was Wilson.

He wouldn't have had a long walk, either. His apartment was only a few blocks from Capitol Hill, though he'd have had a bit of a hike to reach the outer lying restaurants where his "target audience," as he called them, partook of long, liquor-laden lunches. But Wilson eschewed the concrete pathways that made up DC's sidewalks. He drove or cabbed or hitched rides with the men and women who looked after the business of the country.

It started when he was in school, in second grade. He and his classmates had been playing "Step on a Crack" and, with his tiny feet, he'd won hands down. Everyone else trod on those insidious little lines that webbed across the concrete, but not Wilson. Everyone tried to beat him but no one could. Not until school was almost over, in May.

He'd grown careless, too sure of himself. And he'd stepped on a crack, lost the game. He'd been humiliated and slunk home in shame. Home, where tragedy waited for him and filled him with guilt. Home, to find his father had fallen from the painting scaffold at work and broken his back.

From that day he vowed never to lose a game again, never to play a game he couldn't win. That's why he was the most successful lobbyist to burst upon the DC stage. Because he never started a discussion unless he knew he'd already won.

Those cracks in the pavement had determined his path in life. It was where his focus was, on concrete. He dreamed of creating crack-proof concrete, so no one would ever step on another crack. But he discovered early on that he had no head for science or math. He didn't understand laboratory gizmos or protocols. Instead, he spent his life raising money to help others research into crack-proof concrete.

He'd married well, in a church whose marble floor had widely-enough spaced cracks that he could traverse the aisle with ease. And his wife's money, plus what he earned as a lobbyist, enabled him to eschew walking and thus avoid cracks in the sidewalks and streets as he plied his trade.

But as the years passed his guilt mounted. It began to weigh him down. He grew moody, unable to sleep at night, fearing the cracks in the floorboards might open and swallow them whole, both he and his wife, as they lay sleeping side by side. He worried that the cab's tires would bring bad luck as they flew over the rents in the pavement. He pushed at the senators and congressmen for ever more funding, so more research could be done more quickly. But the powers that be worried more about terrorist attacks and budget deficits than concrete cracks. They began avoiding Wilson the way Wilson avoided walking.

Eventually his wife left him, unable to bear the burden of a guilt he would not talk about, would not share. Wilson used the phone more, and the computer, assailing Capitol Hill by email, text and Messenger. He rarely left his house. He lived surrounded by brochures and circulars about crack-proof concrete and stretchable pavements until the authorities broke down the door and took him to the looney bin. He shouted all the way about the danger below the ambulance wheels, and about the father who fell and broke his back the day that cock-sure Wilson stepped on a crack, way back in second grade.

The Irish Bar

Seamus walked into the room and stood looking around for Paddy McCarthy. The place was full as usual, though it was only ten o'clock in the morning. Most of the out-of-work men of the neighborhood spent their time at O'Reillys Pub, drowning their sorrows in Guinness or Killian's Red, arguing politics and pretending they weren't failures. But Seamus had no illusions. He was what he was and there was no getting around it.

He stepped up to the long bar, staggering a bit from drinking his breakfast, and knocked on it with his lodge ring.

"Give me a pint here, Eamon, and put a good head on it." He shouted to be heard over the din. "Ye seen Paddy this day?"

"Not since Tuesday last, lad." Eamon Sullivan set a foaming pint on the gleaming bar top, his palsied hands spilling only the top inch or so. He made a disgusted sound deep in his throat and swiped at the fragrant spill with a rag that had seen better days long before it had been woven.

"Damn bugger's avoiding me," Seamus said, shaking his head. "Owes me a bundle on that last race at Saratoga." He took a huge swig of the reddish beer and wiped the foam from his lips with his shirt sleeve. "You tell that blighter, you see him, that he'd better pay up. Or else."

Seamus pulled back his black-watch plaid flannel shirt, exposing the once-white t-shirt beneath and the long sheath of the knife he wore on his belt. Sullivan's gaze flicked from the belt to Seamus' cold blue eyes.

"Take it outside, boyo," he growled, his own green eyes glittering beneath grizzled brows. "I might be old enough to be your grandpa, but I can still make your life miserable."

"Take it easy, old man." Seamus held out his mug for a refill. "Only dogs shit where they live, and I ain't no dog."

A shout rose from the back of the room where the pool tables stood. Seamus shoved his way through the crowd to find young Mairead Kelly, the pub's only waitress, surrounded by four young stallions. One held her apron strings in his hands, keeping her trapped, while the other three slowly advanced. Mairead's head jerked as she tried to keep them in sight, her fiery curls flying around her angelic face like a burnished halo. The drunken spectators cheered when she threatened to bean Connor O'Malley with her serving tray.

Brendan McLeod used the apron strings to reel the young woman into his arms. He nuzzled her neck and licked her cheek, then slid his hands higher on her body. She screamed. The tray fell from her fingers and broke into three pieces. She reached up, trying to pull the boy's hair. Seamus shook his head, pulled a whistle out of his pocket, put it between his lips and blew.

All movement stopped. All eyes turned to him. He crossed his arms and stared at the group ranged before him, who stood with hang-dog expressions on their faces. He pursed his lips, looked at the broken tray and heaved a deep sigh.

"And where in the script does it say you're to cop a feel, Brendan? Where, for that matter, does it say you're to reel her in like a fish?"

"Well, uh, Mr. McClintock, I was, like, going with the flow. Ad libbing, you know?"

Seamus McClintock stared at Brendan until he dropped his arms and stepped back from Mairead. Her lips quirked up in a faint smirk.

"No," Seamus said, "I do not know. If there's a flow around here, it comes from me, not from the peanut gallery. And not from characters who are basically walk-ons. I'm the writer, director, and the lead. We do it the way I want it done, or we don't do it at all. Now, if you want to be ready to open on Friday—and to graduate come spring—let's start again. From the top!"

The cast members scrambled to obey, because Seamus McClintock was not just the writer, the director, and the star. He was also their professor.

Stealing Candy

Nothing worked out the way I hoped it would back when I moved in with Al. I thought he was the love of my life, that we would be together forever. But forever ended after only three years. Excruciating years, at that. Probably the worst time in my life... and the best, considering what could have happened.

Al was tall, and broad, a solid man about 12 years older than me. A man who I was sure would be a bulwark against life, a safety net to catch me when I failed, as I almost always did. At least according to my mother. Nothing I ever did was good enough, or right enough, for that woman. She hated me from the day I was born, and it only got worse as the years rolled on.

Of course, she never wanted me in the first place. I'm not sure who my father was, Mom told so many stories about how she got pregnant I was never sure which one was the truth. At least, not 'til after she died. I got a heck of a shock then, while going through her papers and stuff hoping for an insurance policy that might give me enough money to bury her—there wasn't one, her ashes are still in that wooden box in the storage hole under the floorboards. What I did find was a report from the hospital over in Carver City, something about a rape kit and a police report, just about 9 months before I entered the scene.

I've never been much good at math, but even I could figure this one out. No wonder she hated me. Maybe if I'd known what she'd gone through it might have made a difference when I was growing up. Doubt it, though. Even knowing why she hated me, that she had good reason, wouldn't erase my need for her love and approval.

And it sure as hell wasn't my fault some dickhead raped her.

I was kicking around on my own, sleeping on park benches in good weather and under the trestle when it rained, when I met Al. Mom had kicked me out of the house when she caught me with Carlton, who she was in love with at the time. Not that she ever stayed in love for very long. She fell out of it, usually, when the booze was just about gone, or the drugs dried up. But she was still in the honeymoon stage with Carlton —never mind that he was closer to my age than hers—and finding him in my bed set her off into a rage she never got over. Didn't matter to her that I didn't want the creep there, that I was trying like hell to get him out. I ended up the one who got out, with nothing but the clothes on my back and six bucks in my pocket. And still hurting from Carlton's version of "making love."

I was sixteen and had been on the streets maybe six weeks or so, dodging both the cops by day and the local pimps by night. I'd pinched a couple candy bars and a coke from the deli and the stupid kid behind the counter was chasing me when I smacked right into Al. He grabbed me, put a hand on my mouth and swung me into the dark shadows in the alley, holding me still as the kid raced past and vanished into the night. We stood there, him breathing into my ear, until the clerk gave up and went back to the store he'd left vulnerable to all the other petty thieves out there, then Al dropped his hand and turned me around to face him.

"If you're gonna steal food, at least make it somewhat nutritious," he said, taking the candy from my hand.

Then he kissed me and I was hooked.

Mardi Gras Girl

Nothing ever worked out the way I hoped it would when I was young. Not that I'm old now, even though I feel ancient. Twenty-seven is prime time, according to my best friend, Sarah Jane, even though I haven't much energy or zest for living. She says that will pass, but then she's an optimist. I've been waiting for almost nine years and the cloud of pain and misery is still clinging close.

Not that it's all gloom and doom, my life. Mostly it's pretty good, at least nowadays. I have my own apartment and a balcony that overlooks the main street and all the fun during Mardi Gras. I've even been known to fling a few handfuls of beaded necklaces into the crowds below. It's exhilarating, mainly because no one can see me clearly in the dark night, with lights strobing and every-one drunk. During Mardi Gras I'm just one of any number of revelers, people who celebrate their uniqueness. A Mardi Gras Girl. I fit into the dark and the anonymity. You could even say I belong, in a way.

But life is more than a week of revelry; there are fifty-one other weeks to live through. Weeks when it isn't dark and I'm not anonymous. When I don't fit in. When different is merely lonely and alone.

Things were fine for the first few years of my life. I lived with my parents, my two sisters, and my brother, Gerald. He was three years older than me, Daddy's precious boy who could do no wrong, even though that was all he did—wrong. He hated me, I think because I usurped his place as the "only." He didn't mind Krissie and Belle, the twins, who came after me, because I'd already broken the framework of his life, and that allowed for other changes. But I bore the brunt of his malice and my parents did nothing to stop his cruelty.

It mostly took subtle forms: breaking the arms of my dolls and shredding their clothes; giving my cat away to a family on the other side of town; cutting the buttons off my blouses and dresses. Mother thought it cute the way he'd put his arm around me when we were in the park. She believed he was trying to protect me, as a big brother should. I was the one scolded for flinching away from his pinching fingers and for crying. I never knew where my mother thought the bruises came from, but she spanked me the first time I told her what Gerald had done, punished me for telling such heinous falsehoods against her little angel. Father pretty much gave up on me after that. He said there was no point in listening to a liar about anything.

Gerald's cruelty grew through the years, especially when he realized he could get away with almost anything where I was concerned. And he knew he could manipulate me so easily, simply by threatening Krissie or Belle. I cringe sometimes when I think of what I willingly endured; he even went so far as to almost drown me in the bayou behind the house. But I'd do it all again to save my sisters. At least they had a childhood.

I was twelve when things got out of hand. Gerald was fifteen, quite a handsome young man. Girls swanned around him wherever he went. Mother and Father doted on him. And I tried my best to stay far away from him.

Then Father traveled up to Shreveport, to a weekend conference, and took Mother with him. They left Gerald to babysit us girls. I still have nightmares of the look on his face when he turned to me after our parents had driven away. He grinned, cocked his finger at me, and invited his friends over for a barbecue.

I called Krissie's friend, Amanda Portley, and asked if Krissie and Belle could spend the night. I'd have gone to my friend's house if I'd had one. But the kids at school shunned me, due to the stories Gerald circulated about me, the nasty things I supposedly did alone at night. And so I resigned myself to endure in silence whatever Gerald and his friends had planned for me.

To my surprise, he left me alone that night and all the next day. But at midnight on Saturday, he pulled me from my bed and dragged me out to the back yard where his friends stood in a circle, holding torches. He thrust me, clad only in a flimsy nightgown, into the center of the circle and they began to move, darting in and out, waving the flaming torches in my face. I screamed and twisted, desperate to escape, terrified my night-dress or my hair would catch fire. Gerald stood laughing at my tears, my fear, until they tired of the game. Then they gathered around the fire pit and began roasting marshmallows.

Gerald pulled me close and tried to soothe my panic, offering me a charred treat. But I was too frightened of him, of all of them, and I pushed him away from me. He fell and screamed at his friends to hold me. Then he menaced me with a flaming marshmallow, while I screamed and twisted in their hands. Finally, laughing hysterically, he spun in a circle. The flaming marshmallow flew off the end of the stick, landed on my face and stuck to my cheek, burning my skin, my ear, my eyebrow, my hair.

When Mother and Father returned, Father said what happened was my fault, since I was the one who started it by shoving Gerald away.

And so I sit here alone in my top floor apartment, and venture out only at night, my face half-hidden by the floppy brim of my hat, and wait for it all to pass as Sarah Jane says it will. But the monster in the mirror lets me know it never will. Except for one week a year, when I'm a Mardi Gras girl.

Homework Session

I can't believe I forgot the science project. It's due tomorrow and now there's no way I can get it done, even if I knew what I wanted to do. I mean, what can anyone do in a blizzard except freeze to death?

Now here I am, stuck indoors while a white curtain separates me from a good grade. It's just not fair! And now the furnace has gone out and it's freezing in the house.

Man, I really was right when I said I could freeze to death. There are snowflakes stuck to my window, I can barely see out.

Wait! I know... Where is that flashlight? Okay, now pen and paper... Carefully, carefully, damn I need a magnifying glass. Where is it? Ah, in this drawer.

Okay. This will win me top honors, I know it will. Subject: How many snowflakes will stick to a bedroom window in blizzard conditions?

No, Mom, I'm fine, I'm just doing my homework. Okay, where did I leave off? Yeah, there, in the lower left corner.

Okay, now: 3,442 flakes... 3,443... 3,444...

Another Take

The cabin was isolated out in the deep woods. No electricity, only a fitful fire we'd finally managed to light in the ancient fireplace. An icy wind whistled through breaks in the log walls, and night clamped down on us like a vise.

The blizzard that had trapped us raged on. We sat huddled together telling ghost stories, appropriate with the way the wind howled and the fire cast eerie flickering shadows around the room. Branches scraped across the windows and Becky shivered. She snuggled up against me even though Shelly sat on my other side, the most jealous bride-to-be you've ever met.

I chanced soothing Becky by putting my arm around her. She smiled up at me, and for a second I wondered what I had ever seen in Shelly other than her huge green eyes and model-worthy cheekbones. Especially since her envy-green eyes now glared at me, boring deep inside me.

Suddenly a huge thump resounded against the front door. Andrea screamed. Bill, the cool cop, jumped up reached for the gun he'd left at home, his hands shaking, his eyes bugging out of their sockets. Becky buried her face in my chest and Shelly buried her fingernails in my biceps.

Another thud, this one almost kicking the solid wood off its hinges. We all stood and backed away into the shadows, the girls whimpering, Bill-the-cop shuddering like a leaf in a gale. I could hardly breathe, but I was determined to be as brave as the next man. Easy, since the next man — Bill—sure wasn't very brave at all.

Then the door burst open and a hulking black shape appeared.

Becky screamed.

"Cut!" the director shouted. "Damn it, Richard, I can't believe you forgot the axe. What kind of axe murderer breaks in without an axe? Shut that door. Props, give the monster an axe. Ready? Okay now, take number 3,442... And—action!"

Going First

"Ten minutes!" the stage assistant shouted and Carla's heart rate rocketed up. This was it, her big chance. She knew, she just knew, she would win. How could she not? Her voice had never been better, and she was singing the song she'd written when her husband Jason was in the hospital dying. Every time she'd sung it for people at home, there hadn't been a dry eye in the house. If talent wasn't enough—though she was sure hers would be—then the pity vote should definitely put her over the top.

She clenched her hands to quell her nerves as she walked over to the backstage board to recheck her placement. She couldn't believe the way she'd lucked out. They'd put her last, which was great, because people remembered the last contestants best. And since voting began immediately after the show ended they'd be left with her lovely voice, and her heart-wrenching words, in their ears and heads. They couldn't help but vote for her.

But when she got near the board, she saw her name had been erased, and a woman was writing someone else's in the final spot. Her spot.

"Hey!" She didn't bother modulating her tone. This was no time to be nice. "What the hell are you doing?"

"Don't sweat it, sweetie." The woman turned and looked at her, a sugary smile plastered on her too-made-up face. She had about ten years on Carla and stood about six inches taller than her. Carla's heart contracted and she felt herself shrink from a flood of instant intimidation. Damn, but she hated the way her small stature still made her feel less than she was. A mini-midget, her brother Jason liked to call her. But even so, no Amazonian giant had the right to mess with her placement in the competition. So she put on the "no nonsense" tone that had always worked with Jason.

"That's my name you've erased. You can't do that, the last slot was given to me." The woman raised a stenciled brow and Carla blinked at her superior air. "Can you?" she asked, her voice a bit more tentative.

She began to wonder: Maybe this woman was part of the crew and was simply following orders. Who was Carla to question what the Powers That Be wanted to do?

"Don't worry," the woman crooned. "I put you up there. First. Where I was."

"What?" She was a contestant? Red shot across Carla's vision. Her hands curled into fists. "You're just a singer? How *dare* you mess with the order? You put my name back where it belongs. *Now!*"

"Five minutes!" came the assistant's voice, but Carla was too focused, too angry to pay any heed. "Quiet on the set!"

"It is what it is, sweetie." The woman dropped a disapproving gaze down Carla's curvy body. "And you aren't wearing *that*, are you? Don't you *want* to win?"

"What's wrong with my outfit?"

Carla looked down at her bell-bottom pantsuit in her favorite shades of purple and lavender, set off with swoops of glitter and sequins. It had cost her half a fortune, way more than she could afford, and she was proud of it. Or she had been until this, this *person* had opened her big mouth.

"Oh, nothing's wrong with it." The woman shrugged. "*If* this was *1965*."

Carla watched her smirk and strike a pose, her body model thin with a long arching neck and thick curls that tumbled down her back—her bare back, the glittering gown she wore had less fabric on top than a man's handkerchief. What a skank.

The deep plunging vee in front set off her perfect melons, and the drape of the deep blue fabric hugged hips that had rejected every fat calorie since the day she'd been born. She looked like a Valkyrie goddess dressed for the inaugural ball. Unlike Carla, who was short and dumpy and old fashioned with her helmet of upturned bob and bangs and clunky platform shoes. *Surely,* Carla thought, *she couldn't look like this and sing really well, too?*

Carla had had it. She shoved past the woman and grabbed the marker from her hand—her long-fingered, manicured, dark-blue nail polished hand. God, she hated this woman!

"You can't change the schedule," Carla shouted. "I was put last and I'm going last. It's your tough luck you're on first." She scratched out the skank's name and put her own back where it belonged. "Or aren't you good enough for viewers to remember you long enough to vote for?"

"I'm better than *you'll* ever be."

The woman made a grab for the marker. Carla jumped back and her shoes betrayed her. She teetered from side to side, arms flailing as she wrestled for balance. Her hand hit the skank and she grabbed a handful of her glittery dress, but it didn't help. Carla's feet went every which way and she dropped like a stone, hauling the woman down on top of her. They hit the ground and began to roll. The woman grabbed a fistful of Carla's hair; Carla yanked and heard the woman's dress rip. They struggled and fought as they rolled around the floor, kicking and gouging at each other. The other contestants leapt near the walls for safety.

"Thirty seconds! Places everyone!" the assistant shouted.

Carla was too far gone to listen. No way was this thing, this *dress-slut*, ruining her big chance. The woman kept trying to grab the marker but Carla wasn't about to give it up. She heard something fall and crash. Fabric snarled in her hair and wrapped around both their bodies, making them squirm and roll more violently. A huge rending sound echoed in the vast area. Then a bright light hit Carla and the woman.

They stopped rolling and looked up. They had rolled out onto the stage and torn down the curtain. The audience sat in total shocked silence as if unsure how to react. And a camera stood aimed at them, its big red on-air light glowing.

Carla blew her wild hair out of her eyes and looked at the woman she clutched in fisted hands. She saw with pleasure that mascara had run down the woman's face and her curls had gone flat. One long leg showed through the rent in her gown. Carla's left sleeve hung by a thread and black marker stained her white blouse.

"Oh," Carla said, blinking and trying to stand. "Is it my turn already?"

"Oh, no you don't. It's *my* turn!" the woman screeched, obviously forgetting she wanted to go last.

They pushed off from each other, kicked the curtain away and stood up. The band began to play the show's theme song and they started to sing, each trying to outdo each other, one lilting soprano soaring above the dulcet tones of the other's vibrating alto. The audience broke out into enthusiastic applause, and even though both Carla and the woman, who she later learned was called Tracie, were disqualified for undignified behavior, they snagged a recording contract as a duet act.

They never did learn to like each other, or to stop fighting, but sometimes, when the applause outshone the sun, Carla decided maybe going first really wasn't so bad after all.

Mischief

Kiki sighed as she watched the stream of people flow through the gate.

"Another day, another dollar," she said to Evedene, who floated beside her.

"This gets old pretty fast, doesn't it?" Evedene turned in a circle as the onlookers surrounded the pool. "Same old, same old, every day. Sure wish we could change things up a bit."

A whistle blew, sharp and high on the clear Orlando air. Dirk and Marlon swished past the girls, racing each other to the center of the pool. The spectators shouted and clapped. One little girl leaned over the edge of the pool, dripping her melting ice cream cone into the swirling water.

"For crying out loud," Kiki muttered, "can't those parents watch their kids? How would they like to swim in tainted water?"

Another whistle blew; Dirk and Marlon made their way to the far end of the pool. Joe Tiegs swam out into the center and looked at the gathered crowd.

"It takes a lot of time to train our performers," he said, turning in a circle to take in all the onlookers. "We use behavior modification techniques, which includes offering special treats to maintain interest."

Evedene began chortling and Kiki pushed her head underwater. Evedene came up sputtering and lunged at Kiki; water undulated out from beneath her to splash against the side of the pool. Joe turned and frowned at her. He raised his hand and gave both girls the quiet down sign. They turned to each other and smirked.

Kiki watched the people around the pool as Joe continued his spiel about the water ballet aerobics that were about to occur. Small children caused tiny oases of panic as they zoomed here and there, totally ignorant of what was happening in the water. Middle kids watched with wide eyes and slack mouths, and Kiki wondered if they were fascinated or just brain dead. The teens spent most of their time poolside with cell phones in their hands. *Text, text, text,* she thought. *Like the world will end if one of them misses their next text message.*

But the adults, they really bothered her. They were the ones who should have been enthralled, who should have been analyzing every movement, every motion, every step of the intricate dance they performed day in and day out, the ones whose appreciation made all the work and boredom worthwhile. Damn, some of them weren't even listening to Joe. Or looking at the pool. Kiki nudged Evedene.

"Look at that one," she nodded with her chin, "she's not even paying attention. Playing a game on that iPad, I'll bet. Or reading her email. Let's teach her a lesson about what's important in life."

"Joe will kill us."

"Nah, I bet he'll laugh just as hard as we will. Come on, what have we got to lose? The most we'll get for discipline is couple of days off. Sounds like heaven to me."

They listened for their cue, then swam out into the pool, doing barrel rolls, leaping high out of the water, making sure their landings caused tidal-wave splashes that soaked those close to the pool rim. Then Kiki broke formation and headed for the woman who was still engrossed in her iPad, totally ignorant of the performance just a few feet away from her.

"Kiki!" Joe shouted. He slapped the water with an open hand, but Kiki ignored him. "Get back in line."

Evedene gave a high squeak and raced off after Kiki. She touched her back to let her know she had her support. Kiki's heart did a flip as excitement raced through her body. Now, this was true fun, not that choreographed nonsense they performed three times a day. She shot as fast as she could around the edge of the pool, then zeroed in on the woman, lifted the front of her dolphin body from the water, grabbed the iPad with her teeth and yanked.

The woman yelped and lost her grip. The iPad fell into the water. Kiki and Evedene danced on their tails, laughing in hysteria as the woman frantically snatched the device from the water. The audience roared its approval; applause burst into the air.

Both Kiki and Evedene knew there'd be no fish treats tonight. They'd be in the proverbial doghouse—no, make that sea mammal house. *But damn,* Kiki thought, *that's the most fun I've had in ages.* She shoulder bumped Evedene as they swam back to their chastising trainer, already planning her next rebellious act.

£ife Choices

Sometimes I wonder who I'd be now if he hadn't died, because so much of who we are is tied up in who we were, and who was there to help form us.

Since he opted out before we were both fully formed, I've always felt a gap. Something missing. There's a space deep inside me, one that can never be filled. What should fill it is who I should have been: sister, sister-in-law, aunt, even great-aunt— all people I will never become. There should be birthdays filling in that emptiness, as well as Christmases, Thanksgivings, Easters, graduations, weddings, and births—celebrations of life and loving, of togetherness and peace.

There aren't.

The decisions of my life took an abrupt turn the day he yanked them out of my hands. The day he died. Killed himself. Before, my decisions were predicated on the belief that status always re- mained quo, and I would travel the same path that those around me did. In my naiveté I believed the propaganda beamed nightly into our home via television's fiction: do the right thing and your reward is happiness, a perfect family, and fulfillment.

But there wasn't a right thing—or its concurrent happiness, family, and fulfillment—not for me. There was only a gap, a space, an emptiness that no amount of living, no gathering of years, no other group of people, can ever fill. There's a me that never got to live, and a me that is living who perhaps wasn't meant to be.

And that's the crux. I'm here, me. I'm who I am now because of the spaces and the gaps and the never-meant-to-bes, the things that never happened and the things that did. We are the products of our own actions, yes, but also of the actions of others. We aren't isolated islands. We're all one mainland, merging into one another, growing, shrinking, becoming, experiencing, and missing out.

And living. Above all, we're living, no matter who we are. Or aren't. Living, together and separately. Forming one another, making each of us "to be". Sometimes I do wonder who I'd have been, but I wouldn't want to give up this me, this shouldn't-have-been me, the here and now living me. Not ever.

Tradition

When the dust cleared away the land lay flat and dry out into the far distance. There was no trace of any movement, no sign that anything had passed that way. Except for the oddly shaped prints in the sandy soil, prints the wind worked assiduously to erase.

Victor stood at the window of his bedroom in the hogan-like structure he'd erected years before and watched as the sun crested the horizon. Morning was his favorite time, peace and quiet before the rest of the household woke up and demanded his attention. He'd made it more than a habit, standing at the window to watch the sunrise. It had become a ritual, a personal observance that calmed his concerns and filled his heart with peace.

But today the ritual had failed. This was the first time he'd seen a cloud of dust like this, as though someone had come close in the darkness, then hightailed it out of there as the sky began to lighten. Who had been skulking around his home in the night? What did they want? And who—or what—could have made those prints outside?

Abandoning his post, Victor unlocked the exterior door of his room and stepped out into the strengthening light to examine the prints before the wind scoured them into oblivion. There, those looked like the hooves of an animal of some sort, maybe a horse. And there, two long, parallel, narrow scrapes, as though something had been dragged for a couple of feet. And—he took a few steps toward the side of the house—damn, but those looked like footprints. Human footprints, boots, probably size twelve or thirteen, he estimated. What—who—the hell had been skulking around his house last night?

Victor turned and studied the facade, but he could detect no sign of disturbance, no indication that anyone had gained entry. It unsettled him that someone had invaded his privacy; he'd moved his family out here to avoid the constant interference and influence of society as a whole. And his neighbors as individuals, with all their opinions, myths, fantasies and nonsensical beliefs. He wanted his children to grow up as rational human beings, people who used logic as a base instead of fairy tales and wishful thinking. That's why modern civilization was no longer civilized. People were too busy dreaming of some other person to fix things, to take responsibility and fix things themselves.

Especially at this time of year, when the depths of winter closed down and darkness outlasted the light. The last thing he wanted was his kids exposed to the annual mythology fostered by greedy corporations that forced parents to spend money they didn't have on things they didn't need just to fool kids into believing in something that couldn't possibly exist.

I'd better keep that shotgun handy, Victor thought as he walked back toward the house where he could hear his four children beginning to stir. *Whoever that was had better not come back around again, or he's in for a huge surprise.*

"Oh! Oh! Dad! Come here, look!" his youngest squealed.

Victor raced into the house, his heart thudding. If whoever that was had gotten inside somehow...

"What is it, Samantha?" he said, then the sight that greeted his eyes in the living room brought him to a silent stop.

There, spread before him, beneath a gaily decorated pine tree—one that hadn't been there when he'd gone to sleep—were packages and toys and books and sports equipment. His children sat opening presents, exploring the gifts, laughing, sharing, their eyes huge and round and disbelieving. They looked at him, but Victor shook his head. This was not his doing. He didn't believe in this kind of thing. This was what he'd been trying to shield his children from.

Gary, his oldest at eleven, stood up and walked slowly around the tree. Then he stooped and picked up a piece of paper. He read it, then grinned and handed it to his father.

Victor's hands shook as he read the handwritten note.

> *Merry Christmas.*
>
> *I enjoyed the trip all the way out here, but next year, please, I could use some refreshments after that dusty trip. Maybe cheese, crackers and a little Jack Daniels? I am mightily sick of milk and cookies.*
>
> *Your friend,*
> *Santa Claus.*

"Impossible," Victor muttered as through the air wafted a distant gleeful call.

"On Dasher, on Dancer…"

Serendipity

They gave him the wrong name, and because of that he ended up getting married.

It was the last thing Dale wanted. He liked women too much. He'd never once planned on marriage, never wanted only one woman, a white picket fence, 2.5 kids, a slobbery dog and a nerd-attracting kidsmobile.

What he'd wanted was help with his taxes, and Dale's crowd knew the best tax accountant in town. They gave him the name, but he didn't really pay attention to what she said when she answered his call. He was too busy checking out those two cute college girls with the short skirts on the nearby bar stools.

"I need an appointment," he said, speaking over her words and lifting his martini glass to the bartender for a refill. "Tomorrow, around eleven."

"Uh, well, I'm booked for tomorrow," she said. The snippy tone made him frown; he was used to women falling all over him, the way those two girls were eyeing him right now. "But I could maybe squeeze you in at two p.m. on Friday."

"Fine," he snapped, annoyed that she hadn't given in to him. Not that he had anything to do tomorrow, or the next day, or even Friday, he just liked being the one in control. He gave her his name. She gave him the address. "I'll be there," he said.

"Wear something comfortable," she said just as he hung up.

He stared at the phone, perplexed. What did comfortable clothing have to do with taxes, for heaven's sake?

He arrived ten minutes early, just as he always did—his mother had drilled punctuality into him, and hell to pay if he didn't learn that lesson fast—and sat cooling his heels in her minuscule waiting room. There were those weird round Indian woven things hanging all over, with beads and feathers dangling—what were they called, something about dreams?—and the reading material! New-agey magazines about Ancient Wisdom Cosmology and extra sensory perception and Tarot card readings. It was enough to make his skin crawl.

This was all wrong. He doubted this woman had anything to do with taxes. No, this place wasn't about numbers and figures; he was totally immersed in woo-woo-shit territory.

He was about to get up and leave when the inner door opened. An enormously fat man bowed to someone inside, then turned, nodded to Dale with a drippy expression of euphoria on his face, and waltzed out the door. Dale shuddered at the sight of that behemoth actually waltzing.

"Dale?"

The melodic voice turned him to the inner doorway. And there she was, a vision of glory in a glowing yellow and white caftan, beads and feathers plaited into her auburn hair. She was tall and willowy, with a strong jaw, wide cheekbones and eyes the color of emeralds.

She blinked at him and her full ruby lips parted. Her eyes glinted as she took in his business suit, the briefcase he clutched.

"Ahhh. I've been waiting for you," she purred. "I've seen you in my dreams for years."

She gave him a smile that went straight to his heart and held out her hand. He took it and discovered he'd been waiting for her, too. He just hadn't known it until that moment.

Midnight Exposition

How many times do I have to tell you that you simply can't kill someone that way? Waterboarding? Really?

First of all, it's not even realistic. Not something the average person can do. Have you any idea how to even go about it? Secondly, you'll get caught. It's messy, it'll leave a trail a blind man could follow, and it'll point right to your doorstep.

Third, you'd need a huge space where you could have privacy and quiet. Somewhere you wouldn't be interrupted, not easy in a place as full of people as this is.

Fourth, and most importantly, it probably won't work anyway. It's not as easy as it looks on TV to do that to someone, without screwing it up and they pass out or even die. Besides, you'll get all wet and you know what that does to your hair.

Don't look at me like that. I know what I'm talking about. I've lived a few years longer than you. I'm experienced in these matters. What the hell do you think I was doing in the Middle East the last seven years, embroidering caftans? Trust me, I know of what I speak. After all, that's what I'm here for, right? Inspiration and all that.

Take my advice. It'll be much easier, if not as much fun, to use a knife. Or a gun, if you can put your hands on one. A nice Glock, or a Sig Sauer. That's fast, easy and doesn't take much knowledge. Me? No, I don't have one, not one that you could use. You don't think they let me bring weapons with me, do you? Other than words, I mean. Get real.

Besides, why use something that makes so much noise when you've got some really great carving knives right in that rack on the counter? You spent all that time furnishing the house, so many little details; take advantage of it. It's easy to snatch up a knife at a moment's notice, and if you do it right, you could really surprise him. Say, when you're making dinner, cutting up the roast, and he comes in the door after work and walks up to you for a kiss. You turn, like he's startled you, knife in hand, and—whammo! Right in the gut, and there you are, all teary and trembling and half-hysterical so the docs have to sedate you and the cops will feel sorry for you mistaking him for an intruder, and let you off easy.

What makes you think that won't work? All you have to do is adjust a few things in the beginning. Be a bit more devious, a bit more calculating; trust me, it won't change things all that much. Drop a few more clues early on, use that subtext to ramp up suspicion and tension. Come on, you know he really deserves a good thrust, use the 10" blade, maybe you can reach his backbone in one go.

Well, why did you ask me if you're not going to listen to me? I tell you, what you want to do won't work. Okay, okay, don't listen to me. Don't take my advice. Go ahead and ruin the entire story. Kill him any way you want to, I don't care. Just don't come to me again at midnight when you can't sleep, begging for ideas 'cause you wrote yourself into a corner you can't get out of. I won't be here, I'll be out for the night, at the new little bar down the street.

Sayonara, dumbo.

Signed,

Chiara, your used-to-be muse

City Night

Katie stopped as she stepped out onto the street. *Damn*, she thought. *I should have left earlier.* She hated the dark. But she'd been so immersed in her report, so sure if she got it right she'd be up for a promotion, that she hadn't even realized that everyone else had left. Hours before, judging by the depth of the darkness covering the deserted street.

She sighed, turned left, and began trudging toward where she'd parked her car. Late for work as usual, she hadn't found anyplace closer than three blocks away. That was one huge reason to work toward that promotion. It would get her into the VIP parking area adjacent to the building. Definitely a plus on nights like this.

Shadows shifted across the street and a shiver shot down her back. She'd never felt like this before when she'd left after sunset, but then she'd never been alone, either. It was so quiet this late that it amazed her. All the other businesses were long closed and shuttered and none had apartments above them like those on the adjacent streets. Katie quickened her pace, hoping to outrun her nerves.

A gust of wind swirled leaves around her feet and Katie paused, shielding her eyes. She heard it just as she looked up again: quiet foot-steps behind her. Slow and even, as though who-ever it was didn't want to intrude on her space. She turned to look, but her eyes couldn't penetrate the backness that enveloped the street behind her.

She shook her head and faced forward again, realizing with a start why it was so dark. The streetlights were out, all of them that she could see. Was there a power outage? She didn't think so, the lights had worked in her office just fine. She took a steadying breath and walked on, listening intently for any sound other than the soughing wind.

There! Footsteps again, behind her, soft and shuffling as though whoever it was, was trying not to be heard. *Why would someone be following me?* Katie wondered. *Who could it be?*

She opened her purse even though she was still two blocks from her car, and delved inside for her keys. She should have had them in hand before she'd left the building, she realized now. How often had she heard about clutching a key between one's fingers to use as a weapon, almost a necessity for a single woman alone on a big city street late at night? But, like a fool, she'd never thought anything bad would happen to her.

Nothing bad, like eerie footsteps following her down a dark, deserted street.

Where the hell are my keys? She dug more and more frantically, her heart pounding, cursing the day she'd bought the huge, back-pack-style purse. She had everything in it—except the proverbial kitchen sink—and always had to root around forever to find anything. She kept walking faster and faster, prodded by the echoing steps that pursued, slowly drawing closer. *Oh, God, please, help me find them!*

Her heel snagged on a crack in the sidewalk and she stumbled, almost falling to her knees. She caught her balance at the last second, but it had cost her precious time. The steps were louder now, closer. Terror shuddered through her, a burst of white hot heat that froze the breath in her lungs. She kicked off her shoes, her adored Manolo Blahniks, without a moment of hesitation, and began to run.

The footsteps pounded after her. She could see the car now, an island of safety in the ocean of danger that threatened to swamp her. Not that it would do her much good without the keys. Where were they?

It was no use, she couldn't run and search her behemoth of a purse at the same time. She could hear him breathing now, panting gasps close enough to raise goose flesh on her arms. She tore past the car, heading for the intersection. If only there would be a car coming, though she could see no indication of headlights. *Please, please*, she pleaded, her stomach in knots. She dropped her purse, hoping that the butter-soft Luis Vuitton would stop her pursuer in his tracks. Maybe that was what he'd been after, her wallet. If so, he could have it, and more power to him.

Just leave me alone! she screamed into her mind as she rounded the corner and smacked into someone. They both went sprawling, she on top of a hard, lean body. She lay there gasping for breath, her heart in her throat, certain she was about to be killed.

"What the hell is going on?" The deep voice rumbled up from beneath her. "Are you crazy, lady?"

"Someone's chasing me," she managed to gasp. "Please, help me."

Her reluctant rescuer rolled her off him, then stood up, dusted himself off and helped her to her feet.

"Who's chasing you?" he asked, looking around the dark street.

A tall man came up to them in a running shuffle and Katie shrank away, hiding half behind the man she'd knocked down, clutching his suit coat with trembling fingers. She fervently hoped he was not in cahoots with the bad guy.

The signal in the intersection flashed yellow, then green, casting a dim light over the trio. Katie could see that her pursuer was older than she'd thought, probably in his seventies. He gasped for breath like a fish out of water, his wrists propped on his knees, his hands clutching her shoes and purse. Finally he lifted his head, blinked and managed to speak in between gasps.

"You dropped… your keys." His voice came out in a hoarse whisper, as though his voice box had been wounded sometime in the past. "Didn't mean… to scare you. I just wanted… to give them… back to you."

Saturday Shower

This is what I love, Cara thought as she let the steaming water stream over her head. *The entire hot water tank to myself.* It wasn't that she didn't love John and the boys, it was just that with a mechanic husband and three teenagers in the house, hot water was always at a premium. And somehow she never had the coupon to redeem that premium.

Until tonight. John had taken their brood up to the mountains on an impromptu camping/fishing trip, leaving Cara to her own devices. She'd read the latest Ruth Rendell mystery, weeded the garden, had a shrimp salad for dinner —none of her men would touch the stuff so she rarely brought it into the house—and now luxuriated beneath a glorious torrent of soothing warmth. *Life is so good,* she thought.

She pulled her head back, wiped water from her face and picked up the bottle of expensive salon shampoo on which she'd splurged. A thud echoed through the closed door. Cara sighed.

"Elmer!" she yelled. "You dumb cat! If you knocked over my perfume bottle again I'm going to douse you in it!"

She listened and heard nothing, not even Elmer's usual answering yowl. Cara was sure that idiot cat understood English—and thought he was speaking it back to his humans. He always mewed or yowled when spoken to. Or yelled at. So why the silence now? What had he done that warrented silence?

"Elmer? Do I have to come out there?"

More silence. Then another thud, and a screech like rusty nails being torn from ancient wood.

That was not Elmer.

Cara froze, then parted the shower curtain just enough to peer at the bathroom door. Had she locked it? She couldn't remember turning the little knob, hadn't thought she needed to with the guys gone. She set the shampoo bottle down, then reached out and turned off the water.

She stood shivering in the cool air, listening with her whole body, but heard nothing more. She started to call out again, then stopped herself. If it wasn't Elmer, she didn't want to advertise her whereabouts. It was possible, maybe, that the intruder hadn't heard the water running, depending on where he was in the house. If it was Elmer, she'd simply have to kill him once she gathered her wits together and warmed up enough to move.

A scrape echoed through the door. Cara jumped and almost slipped on the water-slick tub surface. It sounded like furniture being moved around, perhaps down the hall in the living room. Cara stepped from the tub and grabbed a towel, her mind sorting through her options. She'd been using the boys' bathroom because it was the biggest. That meant the nearest phone was either in the master bedroom or the kitchen. She found it quite unforunate that both the kitchen and the master bedroom were off the living room, since that meant she'd have to go to the right, in the direction of the noises. Not smart.

What, then? She finished toweling herself off, slid on her robe, and stepped into her slippers. The boys' bedrooms lay to the left of the room she was in. If she headed there, she might be able to open a window and slink out without being caught. She'd be a sight running to the neighbors' house in her husband's plaid robe and her fuzzy kitty slippers, but she'd not let pride stand in the way of her safety.

She cracked the bathroom door and peered out into the hallway. Dark shadows hid any possible movement. Why hadn't she turned on some lights before stepping into the shower? She should have known better, especially after reading a Ruth Rendell tale. Another scrape and thud sounded from the living room, propelling her into the hall to the left, toward the closest of her boys' rooms.

She took no more than five steps before eerie movement near Jason's room froze her in place. A low grunt rolled toward her; glass shattered in the room behind the intruder. Cara caught a glimmer of light as the dark shadow stalked toward her. Her heart thudded. She could barely draw breath. She tried to speak, to plead for mercy, but the words strangled in her throat. She backed slowly down the hall toward the living room, pursued by the menacing phantom. Another appeared behind it, adding his deep growl to the threat.

Cara whimpered as she backed into the living room, certain she was about to be assaulted, perhaps killed. The noises behind her in the living room grew louder: books sliding from the desk to the floor; a lamp crashing onto its side; furniture knocked askew on the hardwood floor. How many of them were there? What were they looking for? Where, damn it, was the phone?

Something—a chair arm, someone's hand?—snagged her robe and Cara screamed. All around her the dark shadows reared; the intruders screeched back at her. Cara hit at the nearest body, thrusting it aside. She raced through the gap toward the kitchen, barely aware of the cool breeze blowing in from somewhere. She hit the light switch just inside the kitchen doorway and spun in a circle, seeking the phone. She snatched it up and dialled 9-1-1 as she ran toward the back sliding door.

It was open; only the screen stretched across the opening, a screen in which gaped a huge hole. Cara turned just as voice enquired about her emergency. She froze, blinked, then continued stepping slowly back toward the screen door and the deck outside.

"Yes, please, I need animal control. A pack of huge raccoons broke in through my back door and are running rampant in the house. Please, hurry!"

And just how was she going to explain to her four men that she'd left the back door open while she took a shower in the dead of night?

Miracle Painting

They never knew who the artist was, there was no signature, but the painting took the world by storm. Someone snapped a photo of it with their iPhone at the small art festival where it was unveiled and uploaded it to his Facebook page. It was just his way of letting his friends know how he had spent the day with his girlfriend, what he was willing to suffer through for love. But the photo sparked people's imaginations and within hours it went viral.

Everyone saw something different in the brush strokes and swirls of paint. Rainbows, birds flying over the water, the sun sinking into the ocean, elk and deer grazing on diminishing meadowlands. The painting seemed to change depending on the eyes that beheld it; the phenomenon was discussed for months. One person saw a mother clasping her dying child; another, standing beside that witness, saw two puppies cavorting with a toddler. No one knew how the painting had been created, or what kind of medium was used. Tests were no help; each one identified something different: oils, water colors, acrylics.

The Miracle Painting, as it came to be called, changed the world. People began to understand that they created life, created reality, each in their own way. They started to take pains to create more positive realities, realities they wanted to live in and celebrate rather than live through and regret.

And deep within the forest, the artist opened a vein in both body and spirit and began yet another miracle.

Wedding Day

Marilee stopped in the doorway and stared at Greg, who was finishing up tying his bow tie. He caught her glance in the mirror and grinned at her.

"Not long now," he said. He gave a last tug on the tie and turned around to face her.

"Nope. A half hour at most and you'll be my brother-in-law." She returned his smile with one she hoped was wider, and brighter, than his. "I only hope Carolyn knows how lucky she is."

"Nah, I'm the lucky one. Caro is just... so amazing." Greg's eyes widened and he slapped at his pockets. "Damn! I lost the ring."

"Silly, Andrew has it." Marilee walked into the room. She blinked tears from her eyes as she went up to Greg and smoothed his lapels. "You gave it to him last night. There. You look great, Greg. Fantastic. This deep burgundy is a great color for you."

Greg laughed and Marilee winced. *Damn, I sound like an idiot*, she thought.

"Well, since you designed the wedding clothes, of course you'd say that. And what a job you did." Greg held out his arms for her to inspect his ensemble. "I can't wait to see what you did for Carolyn."

"Ah." Marilee waved a careless hand, praying the pounding of her heart didn't show. "I just designed what I would have wanted. I really hope you'll like it."

"I know I will. Gosh." Greg moved to the dresser and poured them each a small glass of champagne. "Who would have thought when we met two years ago that we'd someday be brother and sister?"

"Not me," Marilee murmured as she accepted her glass. They clinked and drank. "That was the furthest thing from my mind."

"And now we'll be working together, all of us. The clothing line is really picking up speed, thanks to your amazing designs. And Caro's marketing expertise, of course."

"And you, Greg. I couldn't have done it without your support and encouragement."

"Sure you could have. All I did was infuse a little cash." Greg finished his drink, set the glass aside, and then straightened both his tux coat and his shoulders.

"No, you did more than that." Marilee smiled at him and again blinked away tears. "You talked me through the rough times, lost how many nights' sleep to my worries, had how many shirts covered with my silly tears? I don't know what I would have done without you."

"And soon it'll be official. I'll be your big brother and you'll be my little sister. I've always wanted a sister, you know," he added as the organ music began to play, their cue to find their places for the ceremony. "Never occurred to me I'd get both a wife and a sister in one fell swoop."

He kissed Marilee's cheek, then went out to stand beside the altar to await his bride. Marilee stared after him a long moment before she, too, moved.

That never occurred to me, either, she thought as she took her place as maid of honor for her sister and did her best to smile at the witnesses assembled in the small chapel. *Of all the things I'd hoped we'd be to each other, I never once thought you'd end up my brother.*

Fundraising

"We have to figure out what to do," Shelly said. "This has gone on too long."

Bill sat at his place at the table and looked at the assembled group. God, he was so tired of all this bickering. Not one of these idiots had bothered to look at the facts, much less consider them. No wonder they were still floundering after three weeks of argument and pointless tangents.

"I suppose we could hold a bake sale," Jessamyn offered in her usual shy, timid tone. Andrew groaned and Bill almost smiled. After three months on this panel, he could predict with great success most everyone's suggestions, and their reactions thereto.

"Not another bake sale," Amanda said. "It's too much work, you know the women end up doing it all, while the guys sit back and look dumb about the kitchen—no offense," she said, glancing at the men around the table. "Besides, our last one only netted about two hundred dollars. It's not worth it."

"How about a silent auction?" Andrew suggested. "We have to get the roof fixed and we'll need at least $1,500. And that's if everything goes the way it should. If we run into any more problems…"

Bill looked down and began to doodle on his pad. The argument swirled around the table and he didn't bother to really listen. They were all thinking too small, that was the problem. They didn't have any real vision, and certainly didn't know how to think past the tips of their noses. Finally he laid his pen down and cleared his throat.

"Okay, I've been hearing all these great suggestions," he winced inside at the lie, but there was no point in alienating anyone, was there? "but the problem as I see it is that none of them are comprehensive enough to net the amount we need, plus a cushion for the unexpected."

He looked at everyone, noting the con-fusion on some faces, and realized that his word choice might be a bit complex. But that was to his advan-tage. You had to sound authoritative to be taken as authoritative, and since he knew exactly what to do, had been planning this for the last three weeks, it was imperative that they all accept his pronouncements at face value.

"So what are you saying, Bill? You think you can do better?" Amanda sat back, arms crossed. She'd be the toughest one to win over, he knew.

"No, I think *we* can do better. Better than a bake sale and better than a silent auction. I've been looking over all the facts, what we need, what we don't have, and what we do. Here's what I discovered."

He opened the file folder he'd brought, took out copies of his plan and passed them out as he explained how vital their church was to the whole community, the impact they had on the homeless, on keeping the community buying from local businesses instead of the big box stores, the youth activities that had kept kids off the streets and out of trouble.

"So, we'll do a Capital Contributions Campaign and let the businesses help out. Once they know our need, and are reminded of our support, they'll step up to the plate. Andy, I want you to head the committee. You have great organizational skills and can keep everyone on track. Jessamyn, you're in charge of the publicity. No one can write ad copy the way you do. And Amanda, you're in charge of keeping track of donations. With your spreadsheet skills, you're perfect for the job."

He let them argue the merits as he'd known they would, but within fifteen minutes, their egos puffed up from his praise, they all agreed with his plan. As he'd known they would. Logic and facts always trumped emotion. The church would get that new roof in record time, and maybe create a building fund with the surplus, just in case it ever again rained on the Central Coast.

And Bill would siphon off enough for that vacation in Tahiti he'd been dreaming about. After all, he wasn't a forensic accountant for nothing.

The Next Door Neighbor

She watched as the car drove off, taking Sam's spouse away for a long weekend conference. She'd known the moment they'd moved in it would come to this, and she'd been waiting patiently all this time. Two years, four months and seven days. Not that she was keeping track or anything.

She dialed the phone, then took out items from the fridge and freezer as she spoke.

"Sam, hi, it's Karalee. Looks like you're batching it for a few days, huh? How about I bring dinner over tonight?"

"Kara, that'd be great. How about six, six-thirty? I'll have the bar open."

"Perfect. See you then."

Karalee grinned to herself as she hung up. It wasn't that she was such a great cook, though she had planned—and practiced—this meal for months now. But she'd heard the stomach was the fastest way to someone's heart, and since Sam loved to cook and did most of the cooking in that family, she knew a night off would be welcome.

Stuffed peppers. She'd bought firm, large ones, red, orange, yellow and green. Just for variety and something to talk about. She hummed as she sautéed the ground beef, added garlic, onions, celery, carrots, minced golden beets, oregano, parsley and other spices. Then she parboiled the cored peppers while the rice cooked —jasmine rice, only the best for Sam—after which she stirred the beef mixture and rice together and packed it into the peppers.

She'd wear that skimpy red top she'd bought last week—Sam had said red was her color—and those designer jeans with the rhinestones on the pockets. Flip-flops, to show off her recent pedicure. She smiled as she ladled marinara sauce over the peppers, then added water to the pan and popped it into the oven.

She took extra care with her hair and makeup, then, the hot pan of peppers cradled between oven mitts, she walked carefully across the driveway that separated the houses. She loved that her kitchen window overlooked their side porch; she'd spent countless hours slow-washing her dishes at the sink—despite having a dish-washer —as she studied every nuance that shaded Sam's luscious face.

"Come in, neighbor, come in," Sam called when Karalee rang the doorbell.

"Here's my specialty."

Karalee held up the dinner and gave Sam a sultry smile.

"Here's mine," Sam said, holding up a bottle of fifteen-year-old single malt Scotch.

"I like the way you think." Karalee walked into the kitchen, giving Sam a bump on the shoulder as she passed by. "Let's keep this warm and sample your offering first."

They sat side by side on the couch, drinks in hand. Karalee watched Sam's eyes gleam as they shared stories of their travels in their younger years. Karalee slowly let herself turn sideways and lean toward Sam. She finished her second drink, then leaned over and picked up a lock of Sam's hair, let it sift through her fingers. A shudder ran through her; it felt right, as delicious as she'd imagined it would.

Sam gave her an odd look, a strained smile, and reached for the Scotch bottle.

"Want a top up?"

"No." Karalee took the bottle from Sam's hand. "What I want is this."

She threaded her fingers through Sam's, glorying in their warmth, their strength. She let her other hand stroke down Sam's face, watching as her intent finally penetrated the green eyes, widening them. Not with alarm, as she'd feared, but with caution. Wariness.

Perhaps acceptance?

"Kara—"

"No, Sam. This has been coming for a long time. You've felt it too, I know you have. Just let go. Let it happen."

She pulled Sam to her and tasted the Scotch painted lips, danced with a tongue both cold and hot, twined her fingers into the dangling curls, felt her core open to bliss when Sam responded, touched her body, her face, her soul.

Hours later, in the dark of the bedroom, their dinner long since burnt to a crisp, Sam kissed Karalee and stroked a hand down her naked body.

"I do love you, Karalee. I never realized how much. And I've never felt like this before. I love what your touch does to me." Samantha sighed. "But what about my husband?" She picked up Karalee's hand and set it on her breast, her taut nipple sharp against Karalee's palm. Karalee could feel their passion begin to rise again. "He'll be home in a few days. How do I explain this to Mike?"

The Muse

I want to write about life, about death, about love and hate. I want to write about you and what you mean to me. What you mean to the world. I want to write and write and never stop, not until the sun dies in the sky and the stars fall from the heavens.

But you will keep me here, marooned in silence, in a place without words, without time, without life. You will keep me imprisoned within the confines of your mind, never letting me feel the wind in my hair or the sun on my face. I will wither into a hard shell, a tiny nugget of humanity, so tightly coiled I can never be unraveled. I will cease to exist, never being seen by others, who will pass me by as though I were a part of the landscape they need not consider because it does not touch them.

You have twined yourself into my soul and remade me in your image, and I will never write about life, about death, about love and hate. I will not write but I will feel. I will feel life and death and love and hate. I will feel you. And, deep within, you will feel me and *you* will write. And write and write and write.

Revenge.

Mountain Rescue

Kieran stretched out on the cliff edge and reached a hand down to where Ella clung to a tree root.

"Hang on, I'll get to you, honey," he shouted into the fierce wind that half-blinded him. "Just don't move."

"I don't think I can hold on much longer," Ella screamed to him.

"You have to! Damn it, Ella, just hold on!"

Kieran's heart thudded so hard he feared it would tear itself into pieces. How the hell had this happened? Why had Curt shoved Ella? And where the hell had he disappeared to?

Kieran inched forward another couple of inches, but his hand remained a few inches shy of Ella's. And he could feel himself start to slide just a bit, and wouldn't that help her if he tumbled down to his death on the rocks below?

He inched back, away from the cliff edge, shutting his ears to her cry of terror and despair, and stood. What to do? How could he get to her without endangering them both even more?

He scanned the terrain surrounding him; bushes and trees crowded close to the path that wound along the cliff edge. A slightly wider path led out to where they'd left the car. He tried to think: did he have anything in the car that could help? Rope? Jumper cables, even? Anything he could drop down to Ella for her to grab onto, with which he could pull her up.

That she could hold onto? Was he crazy? No way was she going to be able to hold onto a rope or a slippery cable long enough for him to haul her up the cliff face. He'd have to somehow be able to grab her, hold her, drag her up himself.

He ran to the nearest tree, hoping to find a branch or vine he might use. Nothing. The bushes were no help. He was reluctant to leave her long enough to check the car, but there seemed to be no other choice.

He ran back to the cliff and looked over. Ella hung there still, quiet, her shoulders shaking. He knew she was sobbing, though with the wind he couldn't hear it.

"Ell? Honey, I need to go back to the car, see if I can find a rope or something."

"No!" Ella's head snapped up. Her hand slipped on the root and she slid down another few inches. Kieran almost dove off the edge to try to help her, but she somehow found the strength to lift her free hand and clamp that on the root, also.

"Don't leave me, Kieran. Please. Don't let me die alone."

"You're not going to die, baby," Kieran told her, though he didn't believe it himself. All he could see in his mind's eye was her broken body spread on the rocks eighty feet below. "You just hold on, and I'll be back before you know I'm gone."

Again he shut his ears to her protest and took off at a run for the car, parked a quarter mile away. He shoved his way through prickly bushes that drew blood on his arms and face, his heart hammering in his chest, until he finally stumbled out onto the sandy verge where they'd parked.

It was empty. The car was gone. Curt had take it and left his two friends there, one to die and one to watch helplessly.

Kieran lifted his head and screamed his anguish into the wind. Then he turned and raced back to where Ella hung, waiting for him to work a miracle. A miracle that now would never happen. But if she had to die, then he'd die with her. He'd somehow climb down to her and hold her, and they would drop into the rocky abyss together. Be together in death, together for eternity.

He burst from the trees and skidded to a stop at the edge of the cliff.

"Ella? I'm back, honey. Ella?"

Silence answered him, silence underscored by the screeching wind, the unrelenting wind. Kieran's heart stopped. He looked over the edge at the root. She was gone. He closed his eyes a moment, then steeled himself and looked down, looked at where she had splatted on the rocks.

She wasn't there. There was no sign of his wife anywhere.

Just Cause

"This is it," Melissa said. She rubbed her hands together in glee. "In about ten minutes I'll be Mrs. Garrett Gallivan."

Serena, her matron of honor, reached out and hugged her, careful not to crush the lovely, lace and sequin encrusted wedding gown. They could hear the harp and violin combo Garrett had hired begin to play the prelude to "Here Comes the Bride". Melissa wasn't really crazy about that tune, but Garrett love it, had dreamed all his life about standing at an altar watching the love of his life walk toward him, accompanied by that boring, oh-so-traditional melody. And, because she didn't really care, she'd given in to his desire.

The only dark spot on this day was the fact that her parents weren't there. Her mother had deserted them a few months after her birth, and her father had died a few years ago. And her grandfather refused to attend. Her grandfather, the man who'd raised her. The one she wanted to walk her down the aisle. He'd looked at her and said, "Not if you're marrying that man. He's all wrong for you."

She shook the pain from her thoughts and squared her shoulders. It didn't matter. Grandpa would come around once he saw how wonderful Garrett really was. Melissa was sure of it.

"You have so much in common," Serena said. "I can't believe it. Just looking at you two, watching you together—I could swear I was looking at one person. You even finish each other sentences."

Melissa quashed the unease she felt at Serena's observation. She had to admit, if only to herself, that it felt strange being so much in tune with Garrett. Their minds seemed to run along the same tracks. They often came out with the same comments at the same time. Their taste in food, in music, in movies and television all dovetailed perfectly. There were differences, of course—like Garrett's love for that traditional Wedding March —but they were so minuscule as to be almost invisible.

And there was Grandpa, who kept calling her, telling her awful things would happen if she kept on with her wedding plans. Not that anything ever did, but he was so insistent that she was making a colossal mistake that tiny little bits of doubt inched their way into her thoughts in the deep dark of the nighttime. Doubts that flew from her head with the advent of the sun, and more tasks to accomplish.

Serena sighed and clasped her hands. "If only I could find someone so perfectly suited to me."

"What do you mean? Philip is fantastic. You couldn't do better if you tried."

"I know. I love him to pieces. But we're so different, Mel. We argue over everything. Although," she added, a dreamy look rising into her eyes, "making up is sure worth it. You know?"

Melissa nodded because she knew Serena would think it weird if she didn't. But she didn't know. She and Garrett never argued, they were too much in tune with each other. She wondered what it would feel like, to actually disagree with him. To bandy words and anger back and forth until they reached a compromise. A compromise that ended in the bedroom. From everything she'd ever read, make-up sex was touted as the very best.

Well, she thought as she walked with Serena out to where the rest of the bridesmaids and groomsmen waited, *if that's all I ever miss in life, I'll be doing just fine.* She shivered as she remembered the way Garrett touched her, kissed her, the things they did together. No make-up sex could ever top that.

They lined up as rehearsed. Melissa saw the best man cue the band, which segued into "Here

Comes the Bride". Melissa's heart began to thud as they marched down the aisle, she on her best friend's brother's arm. Halfway there she paused in shock. Pleased shock, for there her grandfather stood, beside Garrett. She knew he'd come around. She knew he wouldn't abandon her on the most important day of her life. Everything really would be perfect today.

She resumed her walk and ignored the scowl on her grandfather's face. Then she stood beside her love, her soon-to-be life mate, his hand warm in hers, fingers entwined. The minister intoned the opening words of the ceremony.

"We gather together to join this man and this woman in holy wedlock. Let anyone who opposes this match speak now, or forever hold their peace."

Melissa smiled her happiness to the heavens. Not even God could oppose a match so perfect in every way. Beside them, her grandfather stirred.

"I oppose this marriage," he said. Melissa gaped at him.

"Grandpa, don't!" she cried.

"I have to, Mellie, I can't let this go through. I can't let you do this." He turned to the minister. "She can't marry this man. He's her brother. Her twin brother, who was stolen at birth by their mother. That's why they are so perfectly suited. They're twins."

Twenty-Seven Paper Clips

Twenty-seven paperclips lined the window ledge beside her, marched in military precision from left to right. Sandy stared at them, wondering who had put them there. How did they get them so straight, in such perfect alignment? How long had it taken? She couldn't imagine even trying to duplicate such a feat, she who couldn't draw a straight line to save her life.

And why was she even thinking about this? She wasn't here to monitor paperclip assembly lines, she was here to fill in paperwork, papers that clips like these would hold together until they were completed, rubber stamped and filed in a deep dungeon somewhere with others like them.

She was here to put her husband in jail.

She glanced around the, well, she supposed it was called a squad room, though it didn't look like the ones she saw on television. This room was cheerful in its own way; two rows of desks, half of which were occupied by men and women in what appeared to her to be casual dress. Not a uniform among them, nor an undercover officer masquerading as a disreputable bum with shaggy hair and filthy clothes. No "perps" being paraded through on the way to what she'd heard was called "the tombs," with hands cuffed behind them and four-letter invectives spilling from their lips. No, here there was the delicious scent of a recently-brewed exotic coffee, subtle mood music emanating from somewhere above, and muted polite voices murmuring into telephones.

Not at all what she'd expected. Not the normalcy of it all, nor the paperclip parade on the windowsill beside her. She clasped her hands then grimaced at the pain that shot into her wrists. She'd forgotten Macy had sprained both of them when he'd yanked her through the restaurant. She'd forgotten the black eyes and bruised ribs and cracked teeth and cut lips she'd endured for years, until this time, this last time when it all flooded back, every smack, every taunt, every pinch and poke and yank. And she'd said, "No more." To herself. Then to him. And then to the cops who'd pulled him off her.

Sandy sighed again and wished she didn't have to do this, that she could just go home to a home that was what it should be, not what it was. But that wouldn't happen. Macy was in jail, she was signing papers, and maybe when she was done, she'd have peace. She'd have freedom.

She'd have time to line up paperclips.

Just in case, and just to pretend she was anywhere but here, she leaned closer and went on studying the twenty-seven paperclip parade.

Flood Waters

"Don't move!" Gordon shouted.

Anita looked up from where she crouched beside the chimney. She couldn't have moved if she wanted to, her hands were frozen on the cold metal of the chimney braces, the sharp edges cutting into her palms. Rain beat at her face, making it hard to open her eyes. She kept them slitted, able only to see Gordon's dark form silhouetted against the roiling cloud-drenched sky, some ten feet away from her, and water. Everywhere she looked, water.

Not trees and grass, flowers and streets. No indication of cars or trucks, fire hydrants or mail boxes. Only seething, churning water with roof-shaped islands rising here and there, many half-submerged. Was it good luck that their house was taller than most on the street? Or bad luck that they had the futile hope of rescue before they eventually succumbed to the flood?

"I'll come get you, babe!" Gordon shouted over the pounding roar of the water and teeming rain.

"No!" she screamed, feeling the house shudder beneath her. The water rose, lapped at her ankles, splashed up onto her bottom and her knees. "Stay away. It's not safe here. Don't, please."

"I can't let you die."

The rain eased a moment. Anita was able to open her eyes fully. She could see the pain on his face, the anguish that twisted his features, the full lips she loved to kiss, the thick eyebrows she loved to smooth. Lightning flashed above, too close above his head, and she screamed. It forked and arrowed down, hitting the roof next door. She felt a shock go through her, a stinging surge that entered her feet and bounced up her body.

Her hands spasmed. Her fingers opened, then stiffened. She lost her grip on the chimney brace. The house again shuddered, seemed to dance on its foundation. She slipped and fell to her knees in the icy water that climbed up the shingles. Or was the house bowing obeisance to the greater force of nature?

"Anita!" Gordon screamed. He went onto hands and knees and crawled toward her. She held out a hand.

"No, please, you have to live. Live for me, Gordon. Please. Don't let me die knowing I took you with me. Stay there, where it's safe."

The wind rose. Rain slashed down again. A crack appeared on the shingles between them, widening slowly. Gordon stretched out on his belly and reached for her hand. Their fingers intertwined. Again the house shuddered, and then the surface beneath her fell away. Like an iron fist, the water grasped her torso and yanked her down.

"I love you!" she cried as she felt their hands part and the icy water closed over her head. "I love you."

One Last Time

George's heart thudded like steam hammer as he cracked open the stairwell door. Black smoke rolled toward him. His eyes watered and his throat closed up. Backing away, he slammed the door shut before even more smoke could escape. There was already enough where they were.

"We can't go down that way."

He turned to Shelly, who stood behind him, shaking and coughing in the smoky hallway.

"But the elevators don't work. What are we going to do?"

He blinked at her, standing like a lost waif among the elegant trappings of the hall: the burgundy silk wallpaper, the polished ebony doors and trim, the plush burgundy and gray carpeting underfoot. Why did she always expect him to have all the answers? Couldn't she think for herself?

He didn't answer, just grabbed her arm and, coughing, towed her back to their room some fifty feet down the hall. If he hadn't held onto her, he knew she'd have simply stood where she was, waiting for rescue that might never come. Or for the fire to find her. Not for the first time did he wish he'd chosen a better mate, one more assertive, more confident. He hadn't realized, had been too young to understand, all those years ago, that passivity was not an admirable trait. Not for the first time did he wish he didn't love her so much.

When they reached their door, George shoved Shelly into the room and kicked aside the shoe he'd used to keep the door from closing completely. He hadn't been sure the automatic locking mechanism would also be out, and he hadn't wanted to risk being locked out in the hallway, at the mercy of the thickening smoke. Then he shut the door, hoping that it would keep the worst of the smoke out of the room until either the fire was out or rescue arrived.

"Come on, hon," he said, "let's do what we can to secure this place."

Shelly didn't answer. She had plopped down on the king size bed. Her hands covered her face and her shoulders shook. George shook his head as he headed for the bathroom. Wasn't that just like her, to fall apart until someone else did what needed to be done? He couldn't help gritting his teeth as he wet the thick, luxurious bath towels that sat folded beside the jacuzzi tub. It was bad enough that he was caught in a high-rise fire; why did he have to be caught in it with his stupid wife?

"Come on, Shel, help me!" he shouted as he wrung out the first towel. "It'll go faster if we're both working on this."

"Why bother? They'll never reach us. We're up too high."

Her plaintive tone sounded near. George looked out into the room to find his wife standing at the window, her hand on the heavy silk damask drapes. He walked out to join her.

Beyond the glass lay the cityscape, a panorama of roofs and chimneys far below their 27th floor room. Smoke rolled into the clear sunshine, rising from a few floors below them. George marveled at how beautiful it looked, lit by the sun that sparked golden glints deep in the charcoal columns. He hadn't realized that death could appear both menacing and enticing at the same time.

Slow tears dripped down his wife's pale cheeks. Her body shuddered. George's heart twisted. Frustrating as she was, he still loved her, would always love her. He laid a hand on her shoulder

"Come on, babe," he said. "Help me. We can beat this. And if we don't, we still have each other. Forever, right?"

She turned and looked into his eyes, seemed to search deep within him. In her eyes he could see their life together, the sweet soul that had so entranced him all those years ago, the mother of his children, his reason for living. Then she nodded, gave him a tentative smile, picked up one of the wet towels and helped him wedge it into the crack beneath the door. Wisps of smoke still snaked through the sides of the door, but there was nothing they could do about that.

They returned to the window to peer down at the ant-like activity below: fire engines, fire fighters, ladders that reached only to the 8th floor. Then George led Shelly to the king size bed, through a haze that slowly thickened. There was just enough time, he thought, before either death would claim them or rescue find them. One last time to show her how much he loved her.

The Phone Call

I had never seen my dad cry before, not even when Mom vanished. But there he stood, tears streaming down his face. He stood motionless, staring into a space none of us could see, still clutching his cell phone. It had rung during dinner and, disobeying his own dictum, he'd glanced at the number, stood up, and then answered. Just that much had plunged us all into silence. And now there were tears, a veritable river of salt water cascading down his face.

None of us knew what to do.

He left the table without uttering a word, leaving us all too stunned to react: me, my two sisters and my four brothers. We looked at each other, the knowledge that life would somehow never be the same communicated through our eyes. Then Traci, twelve, stood up, began clearing the table even though we had barely started the meal. Not even Gerald, only three at the time, protested. We all pitched in, and in about ten minutes all was put to rights. Dad didn't come in to see what all the silent commotion was about.

I settled the others in front of the TV with the sound just barely above mute and went in search of our father. I found him in the shop attached to the garage. He sat on a stool, staring at the wood sculpture he'd started last weekend, but I don't think he was really seeing it. Tears still leaked down his face. He shook his head when I touched his shoulder.

"It's all over, Jamie," he said. "All done. Take care of your sibs, you're in charge now."

"It'll be okay, Dad," I said, though some-how I knew it was a lie.

I heard the shot in the middle of the night and knew: first Mom had left us, and now Dad. I cried my own tears then, for I knew the government would never let me, at fourteen, keep the family together. I thought that was the worst of it until the next morning. Just after I found Dad's body called the cops, I opened the morning paper and saw the headline:

Janice Mistral's body discovered. Husband Jason Mistral indicted for murder.

And I knew that, no matter what happened to us, no matter what we accomplished in life, we all would carry the burden of damaged DNA forever.

$Reading$ The $Will$

The cool marble lobby was deserted when Kristi walked through the double glass doors. A discreet sign stood about twenty feet away, in an open archway. White letters on black proclaimed: *Edwin J. Marsters*. Low murmurs and quiet laughter dribbled out into the hallway.

It was the last place she wanted to be. These were the last people she wanted to see. Although she supposed seeing good old Ed in his coffin would bring a soupçon of satisfaction.

"Oh. It's you."

Kristi's heart thudded as she turned her head to the speaker, who stood just outside a small door labeled 'Ladies.' She'd heard that nasal voice often enough on the phone to be sure who it was, even though she'd never actually met the woman who'd destroyed her marriage. Not in person, though Kristi had seen enough pictures to recognize this ten-year-older version in red Versace.

Just like her to wear red to a funeral, scarlet woman that she is. Kristi clenched her jaw to keep the words inside.

"It figures you'd show up," Allison said, her green eyes narrowed. "Greedy bitch that you are."

"You have no idea who or what I am."

Kristi lifted her chin and let her gaze drop down all five feet ten inches of Allison's sagging, though still curvaceous, body. Damn, she wished she didn't feel so insignificant beside this Amazon. In self-defense she raised her eyes to stare at the softening wattles beneath Allison's chin.

"You're aging well, for a skanky home wrecker. I always wondered what you'd look like in person. Huh. Funny how your pictures left out the skank."

"Still carrying a grudge after all this time?" Allison asked as Kristi winced inside at her own behavior. "He always said you were like a bulldog with a bone in its teeth. And now that I see you, I can see why he left you."

Kristi let her gaze drop again, to the swollen feet shoved into too-small shoes. They looked uncomfortable, Allison looked uncomfortable, and Kristi felt the first stirrings of pity for Ed's second cast-off. But not enough to counteract the bitterness.

"Didn't stay with you very long, though, did he?" Kristi pulled her purse strap back onto her shoulder. "That'll teach you to steal what's not yours."

"Hey, don't blame me if you weren't woman enough to keep him." Two bright red spots bloomed Allison's cheeks. "Mind your own house and leave mine alone."

"The way you left mine alone?"

Kristi felt like she was breathing fire. She took a step toward her rival, fist raised to strike. Allison took a step back, then glared at Kristi, arms akimbo.

"Aren't you wondering why we're even in the will?" Allison shook her head. Bottle-blonde hair swirled round her face. "Since he'd married a third time, it seems pretty weird."

Startled, Kristi stopped and stared at the woman she'd hated for so long.

"Yes, you're right." She frowned. "What is that all about? I'm not anxious to be in the same room with the merry widow, are you?"

"That bitch?" Allison snorted. "And why read the will here, at the funeral? In front of everyone? Why not in the privacy of a lawyer's office?"

The two women stared at each other. The sound of someone quieting the crowed in the viewing room drifted down the hall.

"As soon as Ed's two ex-wives arrive, we'll begin with the reading of the will," a haughty, slightly-annoyed, authoritative male voice said. *Most likely the attorney*, Kristi thought.

"I'll kill them," the women heard a tear-strangled voice snarl. "I'm his wife, what he had belongs to *me*! Only *me*!"

Allison smiled at Kristi. Kristi looked at the archway down the hall, then held out her hand. They shook, a silent pledge of solidarity in the face of a common enemy.

"Seems Eddie-boy is determined to have the last laugh." Allison crooked her elbow. "Shall we beard the lion in her den?"

"One should always be careful who one invites into the den," Kristi said as she tucked her hand into Allison's arm and they walked together through the archway.

Eavesdropping

"I thought I'd wait a few hours before I kill her."

My hand jerked and I almost choked on my sip of tea. I hadn't just heard that, had I? I laid my book down on the table, picked up a napkin to dab at my lips, and took a casual look around at the table that sat to my right, just a smidge behind me.

Two men sat there, coffee cups looking diminutive in their huge paws, heads bend close together. One seemed older than the other, his brown hair laced with gray. The other one's dark waves gave the impression of youth. I let my gaze slide on by them and craned my neck to peer out the window at the traffic passing on the street, hoping they'd think I was just bored and not really listening into their bizarre conversation.

"Do you think that's wise?" the younger one asked. He shook his head and gulped half his coffee, then grimaced at the heat that obviously seared his gullet.

"What else can I do? I have to make sure, don't I?"

The older man ran his blunt fingers through his hair and sighed. He definitely didn't look happy about the idea of killing whoever this woman was. I wondered if my cell phone would pick up the conversation, but I doubted it would come through clearly over the coffee shop's ubiquitous piped-in music and the mutterings of the other patrons. Maybe I could snap a quick photo of them. Without them noticing? *Never happen*, I thought.

"Dave, come on." The younger guy leaned back in his seat and crossed his arms. "A few hours is excessive, don't you think? You've always been too cautious."

"Maybe you're right, José. Probably an hour is enough time to make sure things are right."

"You don't need even an hour, but do it your way if you must."

"Nice to know I have your approval, buddy."

They sat in silence a moment, staring out the window, and I finished my tea, picked up my book and slid my cell out of my pocket. Masked by the open book, I flipped it open and hovered my finger over the #1 button, my shortcut to 9-1-1. If I called now, the two men would hear me just as I was hearing them. But if I let them leave, how could I tell the cops where to find them before they were able to kill this woman? I glanced at them again and this time the younger one, José, caught my eye. He frowned at me and I made a show of paging through my book. He cleared his throat and nodded at me when Dave looked up.

They rose to leave. My heart leapt into my throat as José came close to my table and stood over me. Surely they wouldn't hurt me in full view of everyone, would they?

"It's not nice to listen to other people's conversations, honey," he said, his tone cold as ice. "Try a little politeness next time. Come on, Dave, let's get out of here."

They walked away. I rose and followed them, hoping maybe to catch their license plate number. But I stopped just before the front door when I heard Dave say, "I'm sure I'll have to let that engine run a good hour before I kill her, or I'll never find where that burp is coming from. I hate intermittent problems, they're close to impossible to find. Damn modern engines…"

His voice faded as the doors closed behind them. And I stood there like an idiot in the middle of Starbucks, cell in hand, 9-1-1 almost dialed, and laughed at myself. Polite, indeed.

Yeah, next time.

Good Looks

"Where do good looks come from?" Dorina asked, checking out her makeup in the high school bathroom mirror. "Is it genetic or something?"

She leaned forward to touch up her mascara, lengthening her long lashes another millimeter. Kaylee smiled at her reflection.

"I think it's the luck of the draw," she said, then applied her brush to her thick auburn curls in slow sensual strokes. She blinked her gamin-green eyes and pursed her full ruby lips in a faux kiss. She knew, with her high cheekbones and fine china complexion, that no one could think she wasn't just the cutest thing around, well on her way to true beauty.

"Well, we certainly got lucky," Dorina said, stroking her long, thin neck.

Behind her, a stall door opened. Hazel Masters scurried out, her body hunched as though she expected harsh blows to fall on her back. She went to the furthest sink and began washing her hands, not even giving her two classmates a glance. Dorina glanced at Kaylee. Her lips twitched into a smile.

"Oh, more than lucky," Kaylee said. "And I think *good looks* are attached to the *right names*, too. Don't you?"

"Oh, definitely. You have a great name, not a dorky one, and good looks just naturally follow. Dorky names—you know, like *Hazel*—result in dorky looks. It's genetic all right. Stupid parents don't know how to pick names, so they get what their stupidity deserves."

The girls laughed, gave themselves one last look in the mirror and left the room. Hazel stood still, staring at herself in the mirror, their words ringing in her ears. She had a square face, with a strong jaw and low forehead. Her thick brows almost formed one straight line over her eyes. Her nose was crooked, having been mashed when she fell off her bike and landed on her face when she was five.

She never knew what color her eyes were, either blue or gray, depending on the lighting or her mood. Her lips were thin, her mouth a straight slash in her face. No cupid's bow for her. Her head balanced on a short thick neck that coordinated with her short, squat body. So un-swan-like, like every other girl's, especially Kaylee Karstairs and Dorina Springfield, who were both tall and willowy. And beautiful.

If I could just vanish into thin air, Hazel thought. *If I could just cease to exist*.

But she couldn't. The bell rang and she knew she had two minutes to get to chemistry class. *Two more years*, she thought as she headed down the corridor. *Two more years of hell, then I can find a hole and hide in it for the rest of my life.* She stopped and took a deep breath, steeling herself before walking into the derision she knew would greet her in her favorite class, chemistry.

* * *

"Kaylee! I can't believe it's you!" Dorina screeched, grabbing the chubby arms of her high school best friend. She'd almost not come to the ten-year reunion, given that she had nothing to wear but worn hand-me-down outfits from thrift stores. But pride kept her from reneging on her agreement to meet once-svelte Kaylee. Who knew Kaylee would now top the scales at over two hundred fifty pounds?

"Neither can I," Kaylee said with a sigh, holding a plate filled with cake, pastries and candy. "I just can't seem to lose the weight I gained when I had the kids. Each one just adds more. And look at you."

"Yeah, look at me. This is what bankruptcy and divorce does to you. I can't even afford makeup, and I haven't had my hair cut or colored in two years. I look like a rag-a-muffin." She held out her hands, chapped and red from hours of scrubbing offices. A tear glittered in her eyes. "And why bother looking good? All I see every day is trash and dirt."

A commotion rose from the entrance to the reunion hall. They turned to see a lovely woman enter. Her brown hair gleamed with red highlights. Her violet eyes glittered. Her compact body curved in all the right places. Full, lush lips dripped with a deep coral color. She paused and looked around the room. Then she spotted the two girls who had tormented her so ten years earlier. She made a beeline for them.

"Hi, Kaylee and Dorina. Do you remember me?"

The two women simply stared at the vision before them, the woman they'd assumed they would become.

"I used to be Hazel Masters, but I use my middle name now. Elora. Isn't that a pretty name? Not the least bit dorky." She grinned at them. "I came to set you straight. Good looks do not come from genetics. Or names. They come from chemistry."

She winked a contact-lens wearing eye, tossed her rich salon-colored hair over her shoulder, raised her laser-modified thin brows, air kissed with collagen-enhanced, color-tattooed lips, stuck her plastic-surgery-enhanced nose in the air, and spun away to reap the attention of the male population of the room with her implant-enhanced breasts. Kaylee and Dornia looked at each other in shock.

"I knew I should have paid more attention in chem class," Dorina whispered.

"Damn chemistry," Kaylee added. Then they both went home.

Boarding School

They divided us by the color notebook we carried, at that school my parents had sent me to. Red, blue, green and orange, each one a flag that isolated us into separate groups. None of us had any idea what it really meant. Not until our new principal arrived on campus.

The General. That's the way everyone referred to him, each word capitalized as if to emphasize his importance. As if we wouldn't have known simply by his presence. He stood over six and a half feet tall, with shoulders so broad I wondered how he could fit through doorways, and muscles that bulged out his sleeves. His dark hair had been buzzed to within a quarter inch of his scalp; his long, square-jawed face looked like it had been carved from granite. He stalked around campus, seeming to be everywhere at once. We couldn't move without him seeing, and writing everything down in his black notebook. Hard beady eyes glared out at us as though we'd been found lacking in his assessment. Little did I know how true this was.

He sent for me the third week after he'd arrived.

"Aislin," he barked at me in a deep voice that sent ripples through my body. "Sit."

He pointed. I blinked at him from where I stood near the door, then quickly moved to sit in the chair in front of his desk, set precisely at its center. He raked his gaze down my body, then returned to scrutinizing the file on his desk. It was the only thing that marred its huge, gleaming mahogany surface. To me it seemed like a disgusting blemish foisted on perfection.

"You're in the Red unit?"

I was so frightened to be alone with this behemoth that I sat silent, waiting for doom to befall me. I hadn't realized he'd said it as a question—since I held the red colored notebook in front of me like a shield—until he looked up and pierced me again with his glare.

"Are you a mute?"

I shook my head, unable to utter a sound.

"Then what's your problem, girl? Answer the question!" he roared.

"I - I." Damn, I was so terrified of this man, so terrified to be alone in a room with him, a room with a closed door that, I could swear, had locked behind me after I'd entered, that my mind stayed completely blank.

"Do I have to move you? I don't think you'd like being part of the orange unit."

We stared at each other as I tried to decipher the covert threat in his words. What he called "units" were just study groups, weren't they? Or did the notebook colors have more significance than any of us realized? Just who the hell was this General, anyway?

I don't know where I got the courage, it seemed to descend from the heavens. Or maybe rise up from hell, who knows? But somehow the fear fell away—or rather, benumbed itself—my spine straightened, and I lifted my chin. Enough was enough. I didn't care anymore what might happen. Maybe he'd kick me out and I could go home, where there was no General.

"What the hell is going on? Why are you trying to scare me? You don't have any right to treat me like this."

He grinned at me and my heart quailed. But I kept my stare on him, straight into his dead-looking eyes, my chin high, hoping my shaking hands didn't betray my terror.

"You're a jerk, you know that? Stalking around campus like you own the world. Making us all feel like pieces of shit. 'The General'—what a crock. You're the shit, not us. I'm leaving."

I stood and he smacked his hand on the desk.

"Sit down!"

I sank back onto the chair, afraid to even breathe. He grinned again and nodded.

"Brilliant mind, brave as hell, and a smart mouth, that's what I was told. You'll do. Gold unit."

He pressed a button on the underside of the desk. The door opened and two men came in. One yanked me up from the chair; the other pressed a sweet-smelling cloth over my face. Struggling was useless; in less than five seconds my world went black.

The High Ground

Joe sat at the computer and thought. He was sure he could do what needed to be done—after all, he was a genius, right?—but if Rachael found out, there'd be hell to pay. She always took the moral high ground, even when there wasn't any ground to speak of under her feet.

But someone had to deal with this situation, and who better than he? He'd always arbitrated arguments out on the playground, ever since Andy and Mark had that shoving match in second grade. Armed with a superior sense of right and wrong—a trait he'd been born with according to his mother—he'd made them both see sense, talk out their squabble and shake hands. They were still friends to this day.

And so the pattern had been set. By the time he reached middle school, he'd begun advis-ing the teachers whenever tempers flared. Not that many of them appreciated his efforts, though a few saw his innate wisdom. In high school he'd started a peer counseling group, and mentored classmates all through his four years, leaving behind a detailed instruction booklet to make sure someone continued on the path he'd blazed.

This, though—this was almost more than he could handle. Correction, should *have* to handle. There wasn't anything on earth he *couldn't* handle. But this situation would take some really clever maneuvering on his part. He knew very few would understand what, or even why it needed to be done.

The world is filled with human sheep, he thought as he logged on, using the alias account that bounced around the world about twenty times, foiling all attempts to track it. *I'm so glad I'm not one of them.*

He located and searched the target site, then hacked into both the bank's accounts and the IRS. It took about fifteen minutes total to find what he needed—he was that good. He downloaded and altered the reports, copied them to a thumb drive, and erased all trace of both on his computer. Then he made the call.

"Al's Garage," answered a raspy smoker's voice.

"I got it," was all Joe said. "Meet me in an hour at North and First."

He had dinner simmering and drinks waiting that night when Rachael got home from work. As they ate, she told him all about her day at the shop, the two homeless women she'd bought sweaters for out of her own meager earnings—and he loved her all the more for her generosity—then they settled in front of the TV. A breaking story headed the newscast: the front-runner in the presidential campaign had been outed for cheating on his taxes. Copies of his bank records and his tax returns proved his duplicity, and belied his protestations of innocence.

"I can't believe this," Rachael said. "I thought he was so solid, so honest."

"Few people are," Joe said, sipping his martini.

Rachael turned to him, her eyes narrowed.

"I wonder if any of it is even true. He sounds so incensed, so insistent the reports are wrong. Did you have anything to do with this?"

"Me?" Joe turned a wide-eyed gaze on her. "How could you even think that? You're talking government paperwork here, no one can get at that. No, someone at the IRS leaked the real papers."

Rachael subsided—though Joe felt she didn't entirely believe him—and he sat back thinking about his own tax return, the fudge factors he'd been using for years. Of course, for someone like him, the rules didn't really apply. Not like they did to regular people. Or to the politicians and people who thought they were above it all. Who thought they held power. They were lucky they had someone like him to keep them in line.

But just in case, he'd check out Rachael's documentation tomorrow, from his own high ground.

Final Notes

I hope you enjoyed these stories. I always find it amazing to see what comes out when I choose a specific opening, or an odd news story, or a topic, then set my timer for 10 or 15 minutes, and start to write. No planning, no forethought, just fingers on the keyboard, letting words flow.

Some of these stories just may be expanded into full-length novels or novellas. Perhaps one of these days I'll continue the story of Aislin and The General, or Al and the girl who stole the candy bars. Or the Mardi Gras Girl, or check to see what mischief Kiki and Evedene are up to now.

And please contact me with any comments, questions, or ideas you might have. I love hearing from my readers.

If you've enjoyed these stories and would like to let others know about them, please leave a review on Amazon and/or Goodreads. Reviews stimulate word-of-mouth, and that is what sells books for us hard-working writers.

Thanks,
Susan

About the Author

Susan Tuttle grew up in Buffalo, New York, and has lived in New England; Lexington, KY; and Ossining, NY. In 2004 she picked up and drove across the country, landing on the Central Coast of California where she lives in a small town whose motto is (yes, she coined it): *Wherever you want to go, you can't get there from here.* She has found her passion and her place there, where the weather is always perfect—even when it isn't.

After arriving in California, she discovered and got involved in SLO NightWriters, the premier writing organization on the Central Coast (www.slonightwriters.org). She has served as board president and treasurer, is the newsletter editor, and offers professional critiques at the monthly meetings.

Susan is also a member of Sisters in Crime (SinC) National, the Central Coast Chapter of SinC (she currently serves as treasurer and newsletter editor), and the Public Service Writers Association (PSWA). She is also the owner of WriterWithin Publications, an independent publishing company. (www.WriterWithinPubs.com).

A professional editor and writing teacher, Susan is an award-winning author who writes in various genres: suspense, mystery, fantasy, sci-fi and young adult. She also has a 6-volume workbook series for writers of fiction and creative nonfiction titled *Write It Right*.

Under the pen name Susan Grace O'Neill, she has published the first of six volumes of spiritual meditations on the Parables, and a book on journeying with Jesus through Lent. Her work has garnered numerous awards and has appeared in Mind Prints Literary Journal, Tolosa Press, Simply Clear Media & Marketing, If & When Literary Journal, The Feathered Flounder Literary Journal, and Central Coast Kind Magazine.

Susan is currently working on a new series featuring Skylark, a private investigator who has psychic abilities, as well as two young adult fantasy series, and several stand-alone books. She lives on the Central Coast of California with her imaginary cat in a house filled with her (mostly unfinished) handmade quilts and (mostly finished) knitted scarves. Find her on Facebook (susanwriter), Twitter (stuttlewriter), and her website, www.SusanTuttleWrites.com.

Publications

Fiction (writing as Susan Tuttle):

Suspense: *Tangled Webs*
                             Piece By Piece
                             Sins of the Past

Paranormal Suspense:
                             Proof of Identity

Historical Suspense:
                             A Matter of Identity

Short Mystery Stories:
                             Death in the Valley

Flash Fiction Stories:
                             Tiny Tales, Flash Fiction
                             Tiny Tales, Mystery/Suspense
                             Tiny Tales, Sci-fi/Fantasy
                             Tiny Tales, Skylark PI
                             Tiny Tales, Romancing the Muse

(All available in print from Amazon and as Kindle e-books.)

Audio Books (available from Audible and Amazon):
                             Proof of Identity
                             Sins of the Past

Susan's short works appear in the following
Anthologies:

Somewhere in Crime
The Best of SLO NightWriters in Tolosa Press
Deadlines: Murder and Mayhem on the California Coast, Vol. 1
Deadlines: Murder and Mayhem on the California Coast, Vol. 2
Tales from a Rocky Coast, Vol. 1

Non-Fiction (available in print from Amazon):
Write It Right Workbook Series:
Workbook #1: Character, Setting, Story
Workbook #2: Point of View (POV)
Workbook #3: Plot, Dialogue
Workbook #4: Scenes, Style/Voice
Workbook #5: Conflict/Tension, Subplot
Workbook #6: Brilliant Beginnings, Extraordinary Endings

Poetry (available in print from Amazon):
Mirror Eyes

Writing as Susan Grace O'Neill:
Spiritual Meditations: The Journey Series
Lord, Let Me Grow: A Journey with Jesus through the Parables, Vol. 1
(Coming soon, Vol. 2-6)
Lord, Let Me Walk: A 3-Year Journey with Jesus through Lent

(Available in print from Amazon)

Books in Process:

Paranormal Mystery/Suspense Series:
    The Skylark Series (Vol. 1 coming soon)
        Vol. 1: *Tough Blood*
        Vol. 2: *Words Left Unsaid*
        Vol. 3: *Death Duties*
        Vol. 4 : *The SomeWhen Murder*
        Vol. 5 (novella): *Dead Ringer*
        Vol. 6: *Taking a Chance*
        Vol. 7: *The Dead of Winter*
    Stand-alones (connected to Skylark):
        The Eyes of Death (Mackenzie Straite)
        Not Even Death (Linnea Keszeli)
        The Unhonored Past (Clancy D'Angelo/Lillia)

Sci-fi/Fantasy/Paranormal Books in process:
    YA/Adult:
        Destany's Daughter Series
            Vol. 1: The One
            Vol. 2: The Restoral
        Demon's Run Series
            Vol. 1: A Deadly Shade of Gray
        Stand-alone: *Impossible Girl*

    Adult Books:
        Stealing Shyon
        The CPW Series:
            Vol. 1: Cursed in California

www.ingramcontent.com/pod-product-compliance
Lightning Source LLC
Chambersburg PA
CBHW051845170626
46807CB00003B/1356